LUNA STATION
QUARTERLY

Issue 042 | June 2020

Editor-in-Chief
Jennifer Lyn Parsons

Editors
Rocky Breen • Anna Catalano • Linda Codega
Angelica Fyfe • Shel Graves • Cathrin Hagey
Sarah McGill • Sarah Pauling • Cait Ryan
Carly Racklin • Shana Ross • Gô Shoemake
Margaret Stewart • Izzy Varju

LUNA STATION PRESS
NEW JERSEY

This collection copyright © 2020 Luna Station Press
Individual stories copyright © 2020 their respective authors

Cover illustration:
The Trevus Lock copyright © 2020 Eleonor Piteira

First Paperback Edition June 2020
ISBN: 978-1-949077-16-2

All rights reserved. No part of this book may be reproduced or transmitted in any form without the prior written permission of the copyright holders.

Luna Station Quarterly publishes short fiction on March 1st, June 1st, September 1st, and December 1st. For more information and submission guidelines, please visit our website at lunastationquarterly.com

For Luna Station Press

Creative Director - Tara Quinn Lindsey
Editor-in-Chief & Founder - Jennifer Lyn Parsons

LUNA STATION PRESS

www.lunastationpress.com

CONTENTS

EDITORIAL 8
Jennifer Lyn Parsons

THE WITCH AND THE FOOL 14
Emily Swaim

THE MIDWIFE 30
Carol Scheina

DEPTH AND MEANING 42
Jennifer Lee Rossman

THE WISH 60
Caite Sajwaj

ACCIDENTAL KAIJU 72
Dianne M. Williams

THE GLITCH 84
Aimée Jodoin

MOONLIGHT PLASTICS 94
Rachel Brittain

MINOR MORTALITIES 118
EJ Sidle

GANYMEDE'S LAMPS 124
Michèle Laframboise

THE WHITE PLACE 156
Dana Berube

THERABOT 174
Hannah Frankel

THE TRUTH AS WRITTEN 184
J.S. Rogers

THANK YOU TO OUR SUPPORTERS 197

ABOUT THE COVER ARTIST 199

Editorial

Jennifer Lyn Parsons

Jennifer Lyn Parsons is a writer, programmer, and maker. With influences ranging from Laura Ingalls Wilder to Jim Jarmusch, her tales feature a rare physicality with details that feel hand-carved. When not writing code or prose, she is also the editor-in-chief of the venerable Luna Station Quarterly. She finds joy in video games, comics books, discovering music new and old, and making things out of wool, paper, and wood.

I've been working with a new writer recently. We talk regularly about the nuts and bolts of how to write, what it means to shape a story, about character creation and plot structure and all the bits and bobs of storytelling. I often ask them to prepare a few questions for me so we have a topic to dig into when we chat. As part of this work, a few weeks ago they asked where I get story ideas from.

This is one of the most difficult questions for an author to answer, not because they don't know, but because the answer is rather esoteric and obtuse when an author tries to quantify it and explain it to someone else.

Stories come from various places. Sometimes there is a contrived idea that forms from a desire to write something. A particular assignment or theme might be offered up by someone else and and author will write to spec.

But more often than not, when it comes to the stories that resonate the most with others, the origins are difficult to pin down. They come from a mixture of inspiration and an esoteric knowing and they're written from a deep desire and need to share this story with others.

These stories come from deep within, from all around, and

various places in between. Experience, old memories, idle imaginings, music, art, movies, all might contain a spark of something new for an author. Even so, at the end of the day, the story must be written.

Flights of fancy, deep explorations of various topics and themes, escapism, plumbing the depths of our emotions, all feed an author's compost heap of imagination. We turn detritus into fertile soil to grow new stories. This is especially true with speculative fiction, where through this lens of the impossible we're able to understand ourselves and the world around us a little better.

It's been said by some that ideas come from a little mail order place in Poughkeepsie, NY. As difficult as inspiration has always been to pin down that's as good an answer as I've seen, if a bit cheeky. However, please do not mistake the lack of an author's ability to pinpoint their source of inspiration as a lack in their abilities or understanding of their craft. This loss of words means that there's still creative force in the world, a force that helps us understand our connection to the life all around us and to the emotions and experiences of others.

The stories within this issue are things of joy and wonder and beauty and yes, sadness and difficulties, too. They're human stories. They're personal stories. They're stories the authors felt needed to be told and needed to be shared and they couldn't not write them. I hope you find something within them that you can't quite put into words either.

L S Q | 042

The Witch and the Fool

Emily Swaim

Author. Artist. Alliteration Aficianado.

You're a fool.

I know it the moment I take you out of your mother. Most infants on this island know what I'm pulling them into. They fight every inch, then screech when I've won. But you don't make a sound. Instead you wear a cross-eyed grin, like getting born is something to be happy about.

"This one's a farmer," I tell your pa. He doesn't listen. He's a clerk, and his pa is a clerk. He thinks it's natural you should be too.

There is nothing natural about being a clerk. You are a child of the earth. Your arithmetic is game on a spit. Your poetry is deer musk in the wind. You have no use for words.

Your parents don't understand. They think you are lazy. They bribe you with honey cakes, threaten you with belts. Nothing works.

I cannot cure you, no matter how sweetly you beg. There are lines even witches should not cross. Instead I tell you to go west. Buy seeds. Work the land. But you don't believe me. You say you can't make it on your own.

So you do not grow into a man. After your parents die, you live on the kindness of neighbors. The baker gives you treats, your cousin mends your clothes, and I let you sleep in my cellar. You spend your free time watching clouds. It is a simple but happy life.

I assume you are happy. That is my mistake.

It is the winter festival, a time of dancing and drunkenness. You have failed the first labor but mastered the second. It is midnight, and you are sprawled on my porch like a dog. I refuse your proffered cup of your backwashed cider. You ask why I live on Apple Island if I hate the taste of its fruit.

"In case Zora comes down from the mountain," I tell you.

You don't recognize the name. Of course you don't--she left the village before you were born. Before your parents were born too. I am the only one who remembers my sister.

She was stunning. Not beautiful--beauty can be resisted. Her charm was more dangerous. What she asked for, the village gave. What she said, they believed. I told them this was witch's work, but they didn't care. She was a flower and I was a weed.

I broke her spell, but even after her true face was revealed, the villagers loved her. So I chased her out of town. The villagers mourned the loss of their princess, but they didn't get involved. They knew better than to interfere in witches' feuds.

Zora escaped to Lovers' Peak and had her golems build her a fortress. She lives there to this day. Her face looks young, but her soul is older than mine. I'm sure she will die first.

That night, Zora takes hold of your dreams. You ask your neighbors about her, and they each tell you a different lie. She is lovely. She is kind. She is lonely.

"Is it true," you ask me one misty afternoon, "that your sister will marry any man who can make her happy?"

"She's said as much. But it's an impossible quest. Her heart is like your mind." I tap you on the head. "Empty."

"But would she marry that man?"

I realize you are in love. Love! With a witch whose only virtue is a beauty you've never seen.

"Don't go courting such a woman," I tell you. "If the earth won't take her, she's not worth having."

You don't listen. When the last frost thaws, you leave. Your cousin gives you a map. The baker packs your bags with bread, and the priest gives you his blessing. Your boots leave a trail of crushed grass, a brush stroke on the mountain. I do not wake until you are gone.

Scoundrels. Miscreants. Selfish wretches. Sending a lamb into a lion's den.

I cannot follow you. My bones are too brittle for such a climb. But a witch has other tricks. I grab my seer's bowl and fill it with moonwater. Dip my face inside. My mind floats up the mountainside. I find you near the top.

Her castle is gaudier than I remember. Its walls are a mosaic of pearl bricks. The windows are lined with gold, and the towers are tipped with diamonds. A tasteless display, especially for a witch.

But you aren't admiring the castle. You are wandering the edges of her lawn, smelling her garden.

It is a good garden, I will give you that. Zora has every flower in the world up here. You pluck yourself a fire lily, and I can smell it with you, a deep, spicy aroma that makes your nose tingle.

Take the flower and leave, fool. I can grow you a garden back home.

You can't hear me, so you don't listen. You keep picking flowers. I dip my hands into the bowl. I tell the rainclouds to fly your way. Perhaps a cold shower will wash some sense in your ears.

You finish your bouquet and knock on the castle door. I urge the clouds on, but the winds are too slow to save you. Zora appears.

She is ugly to me. Her skin is waxy and her hair hangs like a spider's web. The only human part of her is the muddied hazel in her eyes.

You kneel before Zora and compare her to the moon. Then you hand her your flowers, the same flowers you picked from her garden. She hands the bouquet back. "Go home, boy. I have no use for the love of a peasant."

Yes. Come home. She has plenty of servants. She doesn't need you.

You are dejected but smile anyway. "As you wish, milady. May I take a flower to remember you by?"

"A flower?" She is intrigued. "Which of these flowers reminds you of me?"

You pick a sprig of tea olive--a puny plant with wisps of white flowers. "This one. It smells like a summer morning."

I expect her to punish you for your insolence. Instead she takes the sprig. "Does it now?"

"You disagree?"

"I wouldn't know. My sense of smell was stolen years ago."

"How horrible! If your nose doesn't work, please take mine!"

You poor, precious fool. Where else but a witch's castle would such a gift make sense?

She agrees to trade your nose for her flower. She takes you through the garden and makes you describe the scent of each blossom. Your descriptions are more poetry than fact, but she doesn't know that.

She places her finger on your nose. She recites her spell in the old tongue. I know the words, but I cannot stop her. I can only watch and suffer with you.

She takes the smell of your mother first. Then parchment, wet grass, and cinnamon. Everything you ever smelled flows out of your nose and into her finger. The smells pour faster and faster. Your nose is close to bursting. Then she stops chanting, and your nose is dead.

Zora sniffs the tea olive. "You were right. It smells like morning." She hands the flower to you. Of course you can't enjoy it now. What a cruel woman.

She takes you on a second walk through the garden. She sniffs every flower, making sure she's gotten all the right smells. You overlook her selfishness, admiring the flowers' colors and the chirping of the birds. You think yourself lucky, which is all the more infuriating.

You are almost done with your tour. She is about to release you when my clouds, those stupid clouds, roll over the peaks. They dump their icy rain over the garden. Zora, witch she may be, has enough manners to invite you inside.

She takes you into her dining room. Red velvet lines the walls, and a large window overlooks the garden. She sits at the table--you sit at a tea tray.

Her servants come in with dinner. They're eight feet tall, shaped more like trolls than men. Their bodies are a shell of rocks that clack as they move.

My clouds spit out some lightning. Pay attention, fool. Look between the cracks of that one's shell. You can see the fire of the demon inside.

You can see it. I feel you looking. But your eyes are distracted by the tray set before you. Her servants have prepared a swordfish. I can tell from the sweet tang of the sauce--it's the best meal you've ever had.

"This tuna is delicious, milady."

"Is that right?" She dabs her lips with a napkin. "That's a relief. It's been a while since I've served a guest. I wasn't sure my servants remembered how to cook."

You notice Zora has nothing but a bowl of broth before her. She takes a sip, and her sleeves fall down. Her wrists bulge, and you can see a web of veins under her paper-thin skin. She has not enjoyed a full meal in a while.

"You don't eat their food?"

"My taste was stolen as well."

I didn't steal her sense of taste. It broke when I erased her spell.

"How awful!"

"Meals are often a chore," she admits. "But drinking tea with company has been... pleasant."

"Then you should do it more often."

She sets down her spoon. "Exactly what are you proposing?"

Now, of all times, you become shy. "Milady, is it true you will marry any man who can bring you happiness?"

She smirks. "I will admit, boy, you are amusing. But you'll need more than a nose to buy my kingdom."

You finish your dinner. "I am told that a good meal can often lift one's spirits."

"If you wish to try, I won't stop you."

No, fool. Don't do it.

You kneel before her. She places her finger on your tongue. The tastes wash through you, from the sweetest honey to my bitterest medicine. She recognizes that last taste, a remedy I make for fevers. She stares but says nothing.

The servants bring in cake. It is delicious, I'm sure, all cream and chocolate. But I won't let her have it. I throw a stroke of lightning outside her window. Thunder shakes the room. The servants flinch. The cake plops on the carpet.

I've scared her now. Zora asks if you called the lightning. You shake your head--you hate storms. She asks if you apprentice to anyone. You tell her you run errands for the baker. Your innocence puts her at ease. You beg her to have the servants make another cake. But Zora is no longer hungry. She asks if you would like to dance instead.

You can say no. It's not too late to escape.

But of course you say yes. She takes you into a large, round dome. Colors sift through the walls like a rainbow through clouds. Her golem monstrosities play timid melodies on their violins. She takes you onto the dance floor, spinning you around like a top. Watch your feet, fool, she moves quickly.

You watch your reflection in the floor. The marble reflects every grain of dust on your face. You feel nervous for all the wrong reasons.

"Have my looks become so dull in the last hour that you'd rather gaze on the floor than me?"

"No, milady. I was simply admiring the way the floor catches the light. It's like we're dancing across a rainbow in the night sky."

"Does it now?" Zora asks. "I wouldn't know. I cannot see colors."

The two of you dance across the floor's abyss. For once you keep your mouth shut.

"Boy, I would like to see colors."

"But milady, without my eyes, I won't be able to behold your beautiful face."

"Didn't you want to be my king?"

"With all my heart!"

"Then shouldn't you be grateful for this chance to give me happiness?"

Don't be grateful. Be afraid.

You kneel. She touches your eyes and chants. Pictures of your life pour out of your eyes, faster and faster until they're a storm of images. Put the colors to memory, fool. I won't be able to get them back for you.

"The world is so beautiful," she murmurs. "I had forgotten."

Your eyes burn. The world is a patchwork of gray blurs. You can't tell where the wall ends and Zora begins.

"Have I made you happy, milady?"

"I'm not sure yet."

Her soft hands pull you up. She guides your hands around her waist. The music starts up again. She still expects you to dance?

My poor fool, you try your best. But your feet move out of time, and you can't tell where to turn. You inevitably step on her toes. Zora hisses in pain. "Perhaps you are done dancing for the night."

"Perhaps." You are too humiliated to ask for a second chance.

She leads you to the front door. The rain falls down in thundering sheets. To you, it's nothing more than a shimmering wall of gray. You hold out your hand--it feels like dipping your arm in ice.

"Milady, could I at least stay until the rain stops?"

She slips the tea olive into your shirt. "Come back another time. I'll let you try again."

A servant grabs an umbrella. It takes you by the arm and leads you out of the garden. You can barely walk without slipping. Zora glides beside you, admiring the greens and blues of my storm clouds.

I can't save you, but I can hurt her. If I focus my energies, time it just right... Now.

I throw a piece of lightning her way. It almost hits, but the golem throws itself in front of her. The world turns white, and the demon inside screams. The impact throws you and Zora into the mud.

Zora is unharmed. You are scratched up, but you'll live. The golem has been charred into a statue. The demon is gone, freed from its cage.

Zora carries you inside and slams the door. "Was that lighting your attempt to intimidate me?"

"That flash was lightning?"

She throws you against the wall. "Did I not give you your flower? Invite you into my castle? I gave you everything we agreed upon and more. You don't have any right to be angry."

"Why would I be angry?"

"Don't play games with me, boy. That strike was *aimed*."

"Milady, I'm blind."

"If you love your senses so much, why did you give them away?"

"Because I love you more."

Your eyes are clouded over from her spell. She leans closer, though I'm not sure what she's seeing--

"Ariella."

Me. She sees me.

I let the thunder roll. If I've been discovered, then I might as well make a show of it. Let her know you're under my protection.

"I changed my mind, boy. You should wait out the storm here."

You are confused but happy, like a puppy that's gotten a treat for piddling on the floor. "Really?"

She nods. "You'll spend the night in my old room."

She leads you up a long flight of stairs. At the top is a bedroom full of lace and dust. She sits you down on a large feather bed. You look up at her. Your eyes have recovered enough to see the curl of her mouth.

"Milady... you're smiling."

"Yes."

"Does that mean I've made you happy?"

She sits next to you. "As happy as a witch can get without a heart."

Her words chill your bones. You laugh and pretend to misunderstand. "What do you mean, without a heart?"

"I mean what I mean." Zora pats you dry with a blanket. "Didn't I explain this to you in the garden?"

"You have no use for love." You stand up. Stumble towards the door.

Zora realizes her mistake. "But I am happy." Her breath flutters against your ear. "Happy enough to reconsider your marriage offer."

"I can't marry you."

"If I can turn stones into servants, I can make a peasant king."

You back away. She grabs your hand. "Did you not hear me,

boy? I said I'd make you king. You can rule, have all the riches in the world."

"That's not what I wanted."

She pauses. "What else could you possibly want?"

"Your love."

Your words strike her dumb. I don't blame her. Witches look under the surface of words. We skim our conversations for motives and machinations. But she has not lived with humans for many years. She has forgotten how simple you all can be.

"You won't marry me unless I love you back."

"Staying here would be too painful otherwise." You open the door. "I should go back home."

Yes. Come home. There will be no pain here, I promise.

Zora slams the door shut. "Give me your heart."

"What?"

"A heart's an organ like all the others. Give it to me and I'll be able to love you back."

She wouldn't. She couldn't. Zora hates me, true, but she would never take on something so cumbersome.

"But milady, if you take my heart, I won't be able to love you back."

"I won't mind." She smiles--gods, I hate that smile. "It's your choice: would you rather love or be loved?"

That's not a choice, it's a trap. Come home, fool. You can have both with me.

You kneel. "Will you marry me?"

"In the morning, boy. First I need your gift."

I won't allow it. I know you love her. I know it's your choice. I don't care.

I roll up a spear of lightning and hurl it. The floor shudders. You fall at her feet.

"Milady, what was that?"

She lifts you up. "You should lie down. I need you still for this."

My clouds throw more lightning bolts. Zora guides you across the trembling floor and into the bed. My strikes bounce off the bricks, crackling to the ground below.

Zora peels off your shirt. She places an ice-cold finger in the notch of your sternum. "This spell will be different from the others."

The walls are too thick for me to reach you.

"I'm going to need you to relax."

You have to save yourself, fool.

"Empty your mind."

You have to run, now.

"And think of the happiest thought you know."

May the gods raze the world--the first thing you think of is me.

**

My spell breaks. How could it not? There's nothing left of you to hold onto.

I do not wake for many hours. When I open my eyes, it is late, much too late. I hear cheering outside. Something's wrong.

The afternoon sun blazes down. I see you in the village square, surrounded by your now-adoring neighbors. Your crown is too big for your head.

Your eyes glaze over the crowd. They don't see me. They don't see much of anything. Your mouth stretches into a rictus grin. It chills me because it fails to scare anyone else.

Zora stands beside you, waving to the crowd. She strokes your shoulder and frowns when you ignore her. Her love is as true as yours was--desperate and shallow.

She stands tall. Her eyes meet mine, and she grins. She's won.

I turn to the woods and start walking. I do not say goodbye. I do not collect my things. I am a gray, wasted woman, and I have finally grown weary of this island of fools.

This story first appeared May 22, 2016 in the Complex Fairy Tales anthology at Defenestrationism.net. It was nominated for the 2017 Pushcart Prize, but it did not win the award. There are no restrictions to republication at this time.

The Midwife
Carol Scheina

Carol Scheina is a deaf speculative fiction author who also works as a technical editor in the Washington, D.C. suburbs. Her work has appeared in publications such as Daily Science Fiction, Enchanted Conversation Magazine, and Bards and Sages Quarterly. You can find some of her writing at carolscheina.wordpress.com.

"Bloody hell, they always wait too long to call me," the midwife muttered with a thump of her cane and a stiff step into the cabin.

"Language, Hannah," Jobelle admonished, her voice soft as she strolled into Hannah's sight.

Hannah huffed. "Well, Emmilene's not going to care," the old woman tilted her head toward the panting woman lying on a lumpy straw mattress. "She's probably been puffing for way too many hours, from the looks of her. Those ears aren't hearing anything."

The temperatures had risen with spring's arrival, but the damp of early morningtime wrapped around her bones like a stiff cast. Hannah managed to get her body lowered to the dirt floor with a few choice curses. Jobelle gave Hannah a look, then settled herself down on the opposite side of the bed, her white dress filling with air then slowly deflating to the ground. Leaning forward, Jobelle whispered, a feather touch of words into the sweat-laden woman's ear, "Don't worry, she's never lost a woman or child."

Hannah glared at Jobelle.

The young woman in white smiled sweetly and said no more.

Hannah put her hands on the pregnant woman's chest, seeing the age spots and callused bumps of her skin blending into the brown woven dress. The midwife felt the heart rhythms, the pace of each breath. Finally, the swollen belly, tightening with each contraction. Pushing harder, Hannah felt the baby within, and a hard kick in response almost brought a smile to her face.

"The little brat's got spunk, I'll give it that." She massaged the womb through several contractions, drawing a picture of the baby within her mind.

With a creak of the lopsided frame, the cabin door opened, and a young man peered in. "Is the baby here yet?"

Hannah raised her eyebrow and bit back some words. Through tight lips, she tried to sound polite. "We'll let you know when. Now out."

Jobelle said softly, "It takes time. Don't worry."

The man's eyes lowered. He took a step toward his wife on the straw bed.

"Out!" Hannah barked, and he closed the door. Hannah sighed. Childbirth was a powerful time, and she couldn't have a nervous husband looking over her shoulder. Especially when she could feel every second of lost sleep from her midnight rise and trek to reach the cabin. Shaking hands reminded her that her body longed to give into age. Veins popped as she squeezed two fists, fighting the siren call of advancing age, and with a jut of her jaw, she reminded herself, she could not rest. Not now. When her hands opened, they were calm again, and Hannah carefully examined between the woman's legs.

"Water's not broken. Lots more labor to come, it seems,"

the midwife said, the complete picture of this birth forming in her mind.

"You'll need your slippery stick. Pop the water to speed things up," Jobelle said.

"I know!" Hannah snapped back. "Let me do my job."

Jobelle turned back to Emmilene. "It'll be just fine. She just gets grumpy sometimes."

The woman moaned.

Emmilene's husband popped his head in again, his face still long with worry. "Is everything okay? I heard --"

"OUT!" Hannah hollered. She hurled her cane toward the door. It missed, clattered against plank walls, bounced once, and settled onto the dirt floor.

The man's shoulders rose defensively, his face lengthened with the weight of added fear, and he vanished behind the door.

"Don't worry, we're doing great here," Jobelle called after him.

Emmilene moaned louder.

Hannah looked at the cane resting peacefully on the other side of the room. "Devil mother's tits, I shouldn't have thrown that!" The outburst helped as she fought off weak knees and rose to her feet with a huff.

Jobelle watched silently. Her face, usually a white stone of unbreakable calm, had a fissure of concern in it. "Hannah? I've known you too long. Tell me."

Hannah sighed, and her small eyes looked at Jobelle. "The baby's breech. The labor's been long and hard already. Emmilene's heart's too fast, her body too exhausted." Hannah looked at the pregnant woman, who suddenly seemed very small on the straw mattress. "The void is already starting to pull them away."

A translucent tear formed in Jobelle's eye.

"I need my anger," Hannah continued. "The strength's gotta come from somewhere."

Jobelle shook her head. "It always takes too much out of you," she whispered.

"Holy royal bollocks, Jobelle!" Hannah grabbed her slippery stick from her bag and waved it in front of the young woman. "No one's going to die here! You got that?"

Jobelle nodded and airlessly knelt before Emmilene, white skirt exhaling to lie flat on the dirt floor. She began to whisper words of comfort. That was all she could do. The rest was up to Hannah.

Muttering under her breath, Hannah lowered herself before the pregnant woman, composed herself for a moment, and slowly inserted the stick. With a controlled jab, Hannah felt the sac give way, and fluid began to trickle out. Quickly she removed the stick and put one hand on the swollen belly and another on the woman's heart. Hannah's eyes closed and she began to form the cord that connected her to Emmilene, and to the small life in the womb.

The bonds that form between women are invisible, though stronger than oak wood, more powerful than time or distance. As a midwife, Hannah had been trained to form those cords quickly, allowing her to share in the experience of childbirth. First, she began to draw the infant into her own womb, knowing full well the pieces had to be taken away carefully, like sculpting a marble statue. The unborn child was so small to begin with;

she couldn't take too much and risk the baby's body collapsing, nor could she take too little and have too much burden placed on Emmilene.

Beneath her hands, the midwife felt the shape of the baby, forming the picture of the child in her mind. She began to slowly carve pieces away and transfer them to her womb, a sculptor whose work remained hidden within the bodies. The midwife's stomach area, sagging and wrinkled, began to grow, just enough for her to feel her dress tighten. Contractions shook her frame as Hannah also took on the pain, keeping the cord connected between them.

Sweat tickled her forehead as it collected in the two deep furrows aged into her brows, then slipped down her cheeks. She could feel the baby howling in protest, then quieting. "Hold tight, little brat," she muttered. Her stomach tightened in another contraction. She hoped it was enough.

Her legs cramped, her body shook, but she didn't move. The next stage now. Through the midwife flowed the rage of the thrown cane, of aching knees, of trembling hands. She needed her anger, had been building it up to that very moment. Then with a gasp, Hannah released it into Emmilene as the gift of strength. The pregnant woman gasped.

"Push!" Jobelle cried. "Push now!"

"Push!" Hannah screamed.

Emmilene gave a weak gasp.

It wasn't enough, Hannah knew. The void was darkening both mother and child. With her magic, she could see the dark gap, ready to swallow the lives teetering so close to the abyss of death.

They were losing the battle.

Hannah figured it would go this way.

If the void sought a victim, then it would get one. Hannah pushed the last of her anger and strength into Emmilene, and with a sagging stomach contracting and an old body tiring, Hannah grinned. She wasn't done. Oh no. With a deep breath, Hannah gathered her soul, compressing it as tight as she could, and plunged it into the void. "Jobelle!" she screamed. Emmilene echoed the cry.

"I'm here," Jobelle whispered. She'd been waiting for that moment.

Hannah didn't hear.

The void was shaped by a person's thoughts just before the moment of death. "Go into the dark with a smile," people often said, a reminder to embrace death with joy, for the void could be many things depending on one's mindset.

For Hannah, the void was the emptiness of waiting for the smallest sound of an inhale that would never come. It was the silence of a baby that would never cry for milk, of a mother who would never sing a lullaby while rocking her child. It was the dark of a past that followed her, everywhere, and it pulled Hannah in.

The void could be many things, but here, it was hell, and it was winning.

The dark surrounded her, molded to her limbs, and Hannah felt it sucking her in deeper like a black, rotted swamp, the nothingness devouring her limbs, working up her torso, then to her face to steal her breaths.

"Hannah, come back," a featherlight whisper broke in.

At the sound of the voice, Hannah felt a cord pull her from the black swamp, shredding the dark woods, yanking her out of the void. A bond stronger than death. Her eyes opened, her stomach contracted, a sharp reminder where she was. Hannah quickly examined the mother. "Almost there, you little brat," Hannah muttered.

"Push! Just one more," Jobelle urged.

"One more!" Hannah echoed, sending strength through the cord that still connected them, that still sent shivers of pain with each contraction. In her mind, Hannah pushed alongside the mother.

Emmilene threw her head back, sweat flinging into the plank boards, and silently bore down with strength and rage pulled from the cord. It was time. Hannah moved her hands into place before the mother's open legs.

A wet mass of baby slid out and fell limply into Hannah's embrace. Hannah looked at Jobelle for one alarmed moment. Beneath the coat of blood and tissue, the infant was blue and still. Quickly, Hannah breathed deeply, bent over, and exhaled onto the child. All Jobelle could see was air, but Hannah felt she vomited as she transferred the extra mass through the cord connecting them, back into the baby. The tiny limbs grew thicker, heavier, and the small body grew pinker. Streaks of red birth fluids, forming shallow rivers along newly formed wrinkles of newborn flesh, dripped onto the straw bedding. Hannah placed the child on a clean spot near the mother.

It was done. Emmilene gulped air flat on her back, Hannah gasped and leaned back onto the dirt floor, Jobelle watched, and all noises faded into nothingness until there was only the silence of three women waiting to hear one sound above all.

Nothing. Then, like the rising spring sun, lightness came, first with a soft mewl, a hiccup, then a squall that grew to fill the room.

"That's my brat," Hannah smiled.

Jobelle frowned. "She's a beautiful baby girl."

"They're always brats," Hannah muttered, but she lifted the child carefully into the mother's arms. "Your daughter, Emmilene."

Smiling, Hannah noticed no signs of the dark void around the two now. As it should be. "I'm going to catch my breath a second, then let the daddy know. Shit it all, shouldn't've thrown my cane."

***

With the mother and baby well and settled, Hannah returned to her house, where she looked for three things: her chair, a beer barrel, and a mug. There was little else there. She poured herself a full cup and settled into the chair, made of hard, solid wood that forced her to sit at an uncomfortable straight angle. She didn't need comfort right now, though; she needed control. Try though she might, she couldn't stop her hands from shaking.

"It takes more out of you each time." Jobelle strolled into sight.

"Just let me get drunk, have a hard sleep, then I'll be fine for the next one." Hannah willed her hands to still. A small bit of beer made a shallow, brief stream on her lap. "Bloody hell," she muttered.

"Language," Jobelle shook her head.

"You should be talking, you old liar, you. Telling that girl I'd never lost anyone."

Jobelle knelt before the old woman, her white skirt pillowing out. "Just one mother. Just one child. In all these years. You were so young. I remember." Her hand reached out and almost touched the wrinkled face. "I forgave you long ago. Can't you forgive yourself?"

Hannah's hand gripped the cup, her small eyes looked away as her body clenched with the familiar weight she'd born for years. Guilt was a power of its own. It gave her the strength to jump into the void. But more than that, it formed the cord that bound her to Jobelle and pulled her back from the dark every time. Hannah knew she'd be lost without that connection.

Hannah couldn't look at the young woman, knowing what she'd done to her. What she continued to do to her. Yet she would gladly return to her version of the void, her hell, over and over again for the chance to save another mother, another child. The midwife shifted on the hard wood beneath her.

"You were my first," Hannah finally said. "The first mother I'd ever lost. You need to be the last."

Jobelle bowed her head. She knew what Hannah used her for. The cord pulled the midwife to life just as it pulled Jobelle from the void. Still, there was no bitterness in Jobelle's voice. "You have saved so many, Hannah. Let yourself rest. Let me rest."

Hannah's hand trembled as she tried to drink another sip of beer. "I may have saved some, but it's not enough. Never enough."

Jobelle closed her eyes and let the argument go. In a distant part of the house, a ghostly cry sounded. Jobelle looked up and smiled.

"She always misses me when I go out with you." The young woman in white stepped through the wall to find her infant.

The midwife closed her eyes and tried to forget the narrow thread between birth and death. It was always so close. Too close. Slowly, she brought the beer to her lips and drank in silence.

Depth and Meaning

Jennifer Lee Rossman

Jennifer Lee Rossman is an incurable science fiction geek. Her work has been featured in several anthologies and her time travel novella Anachronism is now available from Kristell Ink, an imprint of Grimbold Books. She blogs at jenniferleerossman.blogspot.com and tweets @JenLRossman

I wipe the sweat from my face, leaving a streak of robin's egg blue across my forehead, and step back on my platform. If I squint, the brushstrokes almost resolve into the highlights and shading of a cumulonimbus summer evening, but I can't see the sunlight dancing on my skin yet, can't hear the thunder grumbling ominously in the distance with the promise of rain.

I lean on the cool metal railing and look down the length of the wall where a dozen other pictomancers are hard at work on their sections of the mural. My sister Dex's hair ripples gently in a breeze that comes from nowhere as she expertly sets down layer after layer of paint just *so*, and a small puddle shimmers on the stone floor as another artist perfects the rivulet in his dry river bed.

Even the children, with their heavy hands and uncertain brushwork, elicit a chirp of birdsong now and then as they fill in the forest at the edge of town.

What am I doing *wrong*?

I wave a hand over the control panel, and my cherry picker lowers with a tired groan. It runs just as well on magic as it does on electricity, but that doesn't mean it has to like it. Tech doesn't always appreciate reminders that it isn't in charge anymore, or that it never really was.

Stepping off the platform and walking across the old church, taking care to avoid overturning any of the many paint cans scattered about, gives me the perspective to see the mural as a whole.

It's a landscape, at least it will be when it's done, a sleepy farming town plagued by the drought-of-a-century and bordered by an endless forest and hazy blue mountains. The town is a metropolis now, the forest a single tree in a micropark, but the mountains are still there, hiding somewhere beyond the smog.

Each section of the mural, which stretches from floor to vaulted ceiling and takes up an entire wall, comes alive with the unique style of the artist. Dex's clouds spiral like a Van Gogh fever dream, their wisps reaching out to make friends with Elara's brighter, almost Fauvist shapes. The road tracing through the town winds around Matthias's delicate fences and Carly's bold cubist buildings, trees made of single brushstrokes and trees so detailed that you can see the texture of their bark.

The blank swaths of wall show the sketched-in pencil marks of the elders, waiting for us to paint-by-numbers the magic in. I colored inside the lines, I did everything the others have done.

So why aren't my clouds fluffy? Why don't they take on fanciful shapes? Why are they just flat, cloud-shaped clouds?

The dried paint on my knuckles cracks as I flex my hands, jagged lines of brown skin cutting through the spatters of blues and grays, and I feel the magic course through my joints. I just can't transfer it to the canvas the way I used to.

My head throbs. Too many hours of straining both my eyes and my magic. I go down the aisle between the pews, tracing the footsteps of countless brides and babies and caskets, stopping at what used to be the altar but has become something of craft services for us painters.

Ronaldo, resting on an old plastic lawn chair in the kaleidoscopic light of a stained glass window, smiles from beneath their elder hood. "It's coming along nicely, isn't it?"

I make a noncommittal gesture as I look through the food for something with caffeine. "Not my section. I should be better at this by now, shouldn't I? People used to tell me I'd be an elder by the time I was twenty."

"Elder" is a bit of a misnomer, as most of them are no older than myself. Maybe Circe in xyr thirties. In the old days, when our kind were still persecuted as witches, you got to be an elder by being, well, elderly, but sometime around the industrial revolution, the term evolved to mean the people who were most connected to the magic inherent in the universe.

Most of them end up being outside the gender binary, like me, people who just didn't feel comfortable being forced into a male or female box. I identify on the feminine end of the spectrum and am comfortable with she/her pronouns, but parts of my body will never feel like they truly belong and the idea of people seeing me as soft and nurturing is just abhorrent to me.

That combined with my once-prodigious skills with magic made people think I was destined for elderhood, but something hasn't felt right lately and I can't identify it. Just a nameless emptiness, like a black hole in my chest, slowly expanding and consuming everything in its path.

Not only the good emotions, either. The bad ones, the neutral ones, the get up and go.

But we don't talk about those things.

Society only accepted us witches once we convinced them we were pure, unsullied by negative feelings that could lead to us turning people into toads and cursing their land, which aren't even things we're capable of, but that was beside the point. Those not touched by magic had it in their heads that we can do evil, so we have to be perfect.

Always calm, always smiling, don't let them see that you're human because humans are scared, angry things who let their fear and anger destroy the things they love most. They'll blame this drought on us the first chance they get, even though we're the ones exhausting ourselves to bring rain.

"Your clouds are lovely," Ronaldo says, though I don't think I'm imagining the slight disappointment in their eyes.

None of the food looks good, and only decaf coffee is left. "My head is killing me. Do we have any aspirin?"

They look at me, mouth a tight line.

"I know," I say, "but it's interfering with my work."

Reluctantly, they hand me a bottle from a first-aid kit stowed beneath their chair. I smile my gratitude and down a pill with a glass of water. I feel the spirits dissolving almost instantly in my stomach, breaking free from the capsule and flowing into my body.

Ronaldo gives me a look of mild disapproval.

Most people don't think it's right to let spirits in so freely. I get it. I mean, it's technically a minor demonic possession, and yeah, that sounds unnatural, but there are literally spirits all around us. A hundred billion humans have lived and died on this little blue marble, and that figure doesn't take into account all the animals.

The air is absolutely lousy with spirits. They enter our bodies with every breath; all the necromancers do is concentrate them in capsules and give them a purpose. Once they serve that purpose—in this case, relieving the pounding in my head—they leave the body and go on with their afterlives.

It's not worth having that argument again, so I just smile and go back to work.

***

I wash my hands at the end of the day, watching the water strip the clouds and sky from my skin as they swirl down the sink. All the colors that promise a heavy downpour, washed away by water we can hardly afford to waste.

The drought isn't dire yet, and the city gets its water from a few different sources, so we'll be okay for a bit even if they start drying up. But the supermarkets are down to pre-packaged foods and we're reaching a breaking point. The seers at every paper are predicting another dust bowl.

My apartment is dark, save for the fairy lights glowing dimly along the tops of the walls. I don't dare turn them up; the little creatures inside need massive amounts of water to generate their electricity. Their sleepy ambient light is sufficient for me to walk without tripping over my cat.

I should rest, but I drift over to my easel instead. Its half-finished sketch taunts me, the charcoal rose exuding a faint sweet scent from the canvas. Every time I try to finish it, the smell fades, little by little. A few more lines and it won't smell like anything but failure.

On the walls, other pieces of art come to life. Grasses sway in their own personal breeze, stars twinkle, crickets sing out.

My early work, from before *this* happened, this thing we don't talk about because naming it gives it power. I've hardly touched my supplies in months; if not for the mural project, I might have given up completely.

That's a terrifying thought, that something can so easily sap anything resembling joy from your life without you even realizing. That I could just put down my brush one day and never pick it up again. This used to be my purpose. How did I lose it?

Cassidy, my fat calico, leaps onto a stool and *mrowls* at me. "Volunteering to be my model?" I ask with a tired smile.

The charcoal and paper are right there, waiting, but I don't reach for them. As long as I don't try, I can't fail. Can't feel the frustration of going through the motions and having nothing come of it.

That all-too-familiar void forms in my chest, sucking at the framework of my soul and threatening an implosion. What if this is all there is? What if I can't find that spark ever again? What am I if not an artist, and does it even matter anymore if the world is going to hell and we're all screwed?

I bite my knuckle hard enough to leave red marks that will last for hours, just to bring myself back to the present. I can't let myself get caught in that spiral, like colors washing down the drain, because it won't stop. I get trapped, one tear turned to a night of sobbing into my pillow, my life turned completely hopeless.

I can't do that again, so I force myself to pick up the charcoal and put it to paper.

Cassidy sits for me as I scratch out her form in quick strokes, but my hand moves without any real input from me. Just going through the motions.

The drawing comes together with little effort—I have the talent, I know I do. I can break down an image into its basic lines, get the proportions right and add all the little highlights and shadows just so.

It looks like a cat. Looks just like Cassidy. But the paper doesn't purr, doesn't feel like warm fur under my hand.

There's no life on the page.

***

The next day is Sunday, but the drought doesn't take a day off so neither do we, filing into the old church and opening cans of paint.

My sister and I share a platform today, and enjoy good-natured ribbing as we steal each other's brushes and see how much paint we can get in the other's hair without being noticed. It feels good to laugh, but it does nothing for my magic, and Dex has to point this out.

"Your clouds aren't as soft as mine." She says it like she's bragging, and I know she means no offense but it still hurts. "Am I finally the better artist?"

If there's anyone in the world I can confide in, it's Dexter. She's the first person to know all my secrets. When I kissed a girl in middle school, when my magic accidentally caused that blackout, when I thought I was a man, when I knew I wasn't a man but still not quite a woman.

If I can't tell her, safe way up here in the painted sky, I don't think I can tell anyone.

"There's something wrong with me, Dex."

She swirls her blues and grays into the color of falling barometric pressure. "There's something wrong with all of us."

"Not like this," I say quietly, and check to make sure everyone else is too preoccupied by their own work to eavesdrop. "I'm ..." The word sticks in my mouth "depressed."

The way she turns sharply and looks at me, she reminds me of our mother. Dex's skin and hair is lighter—from the Caucasian half of her sperm donor's family—but those are Mama's eyes, critical and hard, and just like that I'm a child again and I don't understand why I'm in trouble.

"Say something, Dex."

"What do you have to be depressed about?"

It isn't an accusation. More of a plea. *Please have a reason because we can fix that, because we can help if there's a reason.*

I've tried to find a reason. Searched my life for anything that could cause this feeling of impending doom, but there isn't one. I'm at a happy place with my gender, don't want a romantic relationship. I'm not rich but I don't have to worry about money, my health is good, I love my family ...

Yes, the drought seems endless and there are always political extremists trying to outlaw magic, but plenty of people have to deal with this and they can still follow their joy.

Or maybe they just hide it better.

Part of me expects Dex to react badly, to hush me and say that we don't talk about those things, but she's just like our mother. Maybe too much.

"You're so lucky," she says with a small smile. "It might not seem like it now, but your suffering will give your art depth and meaning."

That's what Mama used to say, but she didn't live long enough to reach meaning.

Her depression killed her first. Maybe Dex was too young to know that, maybe she still thinks it was the spirits in the pills that killed her, not how many Mama took, how many she washed down with another kind of spirit.

Well, that settles that, I guess. No way I can talk to Dex about taking anything for this. She might be the most loving and open-minded person I know, but she'll never let me take pills.

Suddenly the world feels like it's going to collapse in on me. I have to get off this platform, away from Dex and her smiling insistence that I'm lucky to have this thing inside me, eating away at my hope and whispering little lies in the quiet moments about how much better everything will be when I'm gone.

"I need more paint," I mutter, though the platform is full of every color I could possibly need. I duck under the safety railing and climb down the cherry picker, not sure where I'm going. Just away.

Out of the church, onto the busy street. I find an empty plaza that should be a bustling market, but no farms have enough crops to make the trip worth the fuel, and I sit on a bench and try not to fall apart.

I don't know if talking about the demons really gives them power or if I only feel infinitely worse because I just lost the support of the one person who truly matters. I just know it all feels so hopeless and those lying whispers in the back of my head are screaming now, and they don't all sound like lies anymore.

Of course they don't need me to paint the mural. I'm not doing any good there, anyway.

Yes, there are people who love me. Cassidy. But I've lost people, and I got through it. So would they.

And what if I never find something that makes me happy again? Is it fair to force myself to slug through a life of pain?

"Oh, child," comes a soft whisper.

I look up to see Ronaldo standing above me, their robes traded in for a tank top that puts all their living tattoos on display and doesn't risk heatstroke in this oppressive sun.

"You're not supposed to read people's minds without their permission," I mutter halfheartedly, scooting over to give them room to sit beside me.

"That would be like telling you not to read a neon sign flashing everywhere you look," they say as they sit. "Your emotions are flashing, Emi. Big hazard lights all around you. I can't help but read it." They talk with the easygoing concern of a grandparent, and I almost forget that we went to school together. "Tell me what's wrong."

"Nothing. That's the problem. There's nothing to fix, so this is just the way I am, and now I've talked about it with Dex and given it power."

"That isn't true."

I frown. "Which part?"

"All of it, Emi."

Those words seem to skip my ears and brain entirely, going instead straight to my heart. I grasp desperately to the miniscule bit of hope they create there.

"This isn't the way you are," Ronaldo says earnestly. "It can't be, because I know you and you're not miserable and hopeless. That's the depression."

I stiffen at the word.

"Depression," they say again. "Depression. Words have a lot of power, you're right. Maybe as much as art. But talking about mental illness doesn't give it power." They point to my chest. "It gives *you* power."

For a second I don't recognize the emotion that jolts through my body and causes me to let out an ugly sob, but I think it might be relief.

"I don't know who first said we're not to talk about these things," Ronaldo says, "and I don't know why we all let the power of their words seep into our minds, but I do know they've never had a mental illness because if they did, they would know the best thing you can do is talk about it."

They put their hand on mine, their grinning pin-up girl tattoo waving to me from their forearm. Petunia, as they call her, exudes confidence and happiness, a testament to the artist's skill with magic.

Ronaldo sees me looking at her and says, "She's not real. Nothing but ink and intention, but she gives me strength because I chose to let her be part of me. We can choose what beliefs we let in, too, and it's important that we don't let the harmful ones in. Talking will make it better, and the people who lie to you about that don't want you to be powerful."

"But what if talking isn't enough?" I whisper, as if speaking too loudly will extinguish the flickering hope in my heart. It isn't that I want medication. I don't. I'd much rather be able to do it with willpower and support, but I need it to be an option.

And ... I hate to even think this way, but what if I don't have time for talking? Mama probably thought she had time.

Is it okay not to want pills but know you might need them while you work on more internal methods of healing?

Ronaldo nods slowly, absorbing the desperation of my thoughts. "It's dangerous to put anything in your body," they say finally. "Food and old world medication included. You can never guarantee the safety of any substance, nor the way your body will react to it." They stare, unfocused, at the passing traffic, introspective. "Spirit pills ... are an advancement that will be invaluable when the process is perfected."

I slump back against the hard bench. *One* time. *One* documented time, a malevolent spirit got past the screening process, was put into a cough suppressant, and possessed a child until she drew sigils on the wall in blood.

It happened one time, and now everyone is afraid to take pills that could really help them.

"And of course," Ronaldo says, "the pills for mental illnesses are designed to last longer than a simple allergy pill. I cannot in good faith condone anyone letting themselves be possessed for an indefinite period of time, but that's a decision you're going to have to make for yourself."

They say it without judgment or bias, but it still feels like there's a right answer and I'm never going to choose it.

***

When the drought got really bad, the Elders devised a grand plan.

Get all the art mages together, they proclaimed. Everyone who can turn paint or ink into something more. Bring them together, and we'll pool their magic to create the most powerful spell the world has ever seen.

With enough people painting their magic with a singular goal, they promised, the mural will do more than stir the air into a warm breeze. More than turn the smell of turpentine into bright floral scents.

The mural will summon a rainstorm. Torrential downpours to quench the thirsty land, to bring life back to the soil.

For a while, as we laid down the first coats, our spirits lifted. We could see the storm clouds on the horizon, hear the patter of rain on the sidewalks.

But that initial surge of hope faded, for me at least. I can't speak for the rest of them. It started to feel like a chore, and the shadow of despair that had been lingering in the back of my mind for years slowly crept its way to the front until it was everywhere and in everything I did.

The pills creep slowly, too. Little by little, each spirit breaking down the walls my brain put up to protect its faulty wiring.

The pills don't play well with my body. Headaches, nausea, dizziness. Painting is impossible, and every cell in my body screams at me to stop, that I'm only making it worse. That I'm being possessed.

But those are lies.

Pills or no, I can't paint, and maybe the physical discomfort is worse, but there's no way to make me feel worse than I already did.

As for the possession... yeah, it's terrifying to let a spirit play around in my skull. What if it's changing me, replacing my personality piece by piece? Would I even notice if I stopped being me?

But here's the thing: I'm already being possessed by something that's changing who I am. Depression is an evil little thing that has taken root inside me, and its only goal is to break me down and build me up in its image.

I am not quiet. Withdrawn. Miserable.

I am not directionless. Without passion.

I am not what depression has made me.

***

The pills have the unfortunate effect of making sleep elusive while simultaneously exhausting me. The days run together in a foggy soup, and I sit awake at night, idly doodling and listening to the sirens of a desperate city.

Riots have begun springing up every night. The thirsty and the water hoarders are at war; it isn't just a farm problem anymore.

I gave as much as I could afford to, but I had a cat to keep in addition to myself.

As if on cue, Cassidy mrows beside me.

"I know, baby," I murmur. "But you don't have to worry; I'll go thirsty before you do. Promise."

Cassidy pokes her head in the window, gives me an inquisitive look as if to ask who I'm talking to.

I sit up straighter. Has she been on the patio this whole time? But then who just mrowed?

I look at the paper I've been doodling on. Just a mess of inky scribbles, for the most part, but there, in the corner ... a cat. A crude, half-smudged interpretation of a cat, but a cat all the same.

And as I stare, it blinks.

Goosebumps prickle at my skin, but I don't dare hope. I'm tired. Hallucinating. That's it, just another adverse side-effect of having a spirit take up residence in my body.

I get a clean sheet of paper, put my shaking pen to it.

The lines are imprecise, the shading and highlights lacking in depth, but I feel it. That tingle of magic in my hand.

I nudge the paper, and the image ripples, sloshing at the edges and turning the paper soggy. When I touch my finger to the page, it comes up wet.

But that isn't ink.

With a laugh of joyous disbelief, I leave Cassidy lapping at the water I've drawn and I run. Out of the apartment, down the street, and straight to the church.

The mural looms in the shadows, sporadic shards of light breaking through the holes in the ancient roof. On the surface, it looks finished, but I can see it now. The gaps in the way my clouds were painted, where the magic doesn't shine through.

I grab some paints and ride the cherry picker up to the sky. In my giddy haste, I realize I've forgotten brushes.

I dip my fingers in the paint, letting the silky blues and whites and grays blend in my hands, my skin giving their colors dark streaks where the paint is thinner. It's a stormcloud in the palms of my hands.

The magic flows from my soul to the mural, every fingerprint bringing the paint to life.

I don't have to force it. I don't even have to think about it. It's as easy and natural as breathing. I can do it with my eyes closed, feeling where each color should blend into the next.

Thunder whispers in the distance. I paint faster, with more vigor. It must look haphazard, like I'm slapping colors without regard for how they look, like I'm just trying to make a mess. But the wall is speaking to me, guiding my hands as they slide through the thick paint.

I'm too close to see the mural as a whole, and yet I can see the entire picture. The trees dancing in the wind, the sky growing dark, the first streak of lighting—

A flash briefly casts my shadow on the wall in stained glass light. The resulting rumble rattles the old saints immortalized in the windows.

The wind picks up my hair, twirls it in the wet paint and leaves thin brushstrokes in the cloud.

My heart is beating in my ears, my breath coming in fast gasps.

A single drop of cool rain falls through the holes in the roof, landing on the tip of my nose, and for a second, the world holds its breath.

I press one final handprint to the mural, and the sky erupts in rain that falls like static and applause.

I can't hear my laughter over the downpour, can't tell my tears apart from the raindrops, but I stand there on the cherry picker and welcome it. Let it soak into me, washing the paint from my skin in a swirling river.

The Wish

Caite Sajwaj

Caite Sajwaj is a writer based in Kansas City. She writes ghost stories and fairy tales inspired by the urban fringe areas of the Midwest. Find her online at caitesajwaj.com.

The day Cressida got the wish, she was on the bus, wedged between a baby carrier and an elderly man that had fallen asleep or else died. She wasn't sure. The bus seats, the final resting place of a thousand ancient farts, were a ruinous eggplant color.

When the bus stopped on 95th Street, the baby carrier was replaced by a young woman, and a man in a thick wool coat sat across the aisle from Cressida. He smelled like the peach cigarillos Cressida used to bum off her roommate in college. The scent mingled with the stench of the bus seats, infusing the cabin with the heavy smell of rotten fruit. *This is what hell must smell like*, Cressida thought.

The bus started moving again. Cressida was listening to the latest episode of the *My Favorite Murder* podcast. It was about Ray and Faye Copeland, a Kansas couple that used drifters to buy cattle, then killed said drifters. The entire thing was about as Midwestern as a crime could get, and just as it was building to a crescendo — the police raid on the Copelands' farmstead — the man in the wool coat spilled the contents of his bag onto the floor of the bus.

A wallet, a lighter, a tattered copy of Neil Gaiman's *Neverwhere*... he scooped all but one item back into the bag. An acorn. He didn't seem to notice that he'd missed it, and Cressida wondered whether the acorn had already been on the floor. Maybe the sudden movement had jostled the clutter that made its home beneath the feet of the bus's occupants. Still, feeling ridiculous, she picked the acorn up and held it out to the man as if it were something precious and not simply an acorn.

It took him a moment to look up from his phone and notice her, but when his eyes fell upon the acorn, his hand snapped out with the same liquid speed that he'd used to scoop up his belongings. Cressida flinched away, afraid that he was going to strike her. She had no idea *why* he would strike her for simply holding an acorn in his general direction, but people on the bus often did things she didn't expect, for reasons she didn't understand. The man snatched the acorn from her hand and stuffed it into his left pocket. *Asshole,* Cressida thought.

He was saying something, but her cheeks were hot, and she couldn't decide whether she was more angry or embarrassed, so she left her earbuds in and said nothing.

That was the end of it. Or so Cressida thought when she exited the bus in front of the Friends of Boone County Library. The winter air was crisp and still, almost painful to breathe after huffing the smoky, rotten miasma inside the bus. She stuffed her hands in her pockets and scurried into the warm glow of the library.

Inside, the ceilings were low, the light soft and yellow, and the air smelled not unpleasantly of dust and mildew. Cressida wound right, through the large print section, and then left, through the children's section, until she stood before a brass plaque that read: *Fiction, Science Fiction, A-E.*

She didn't have a reading list, had really only got off at the library to escape the confines of the bus, so she wandered through the aisles, touching the spines of books, waiting for the one, or two, or three that just felt *right*. She was reading the inside cover of *The Night Circus* when the man from the bus appeared.

"Excuse me," he said. His face was impassive, but his brown eyes flashed in a way that told her he was no less frazzled than he'd been on the bus, only trying harder to hide it.

Cressida took out her right earbud and peered at him through narrowed eyes. The chronicle of the Copeland murders had long since ended and slow, thudding bass emanated from the dangling earbud, as if heard from a great distance.

"Can I help you?" she asked.

The man reached into his bag. Cressida was certain he was going to draw a pistol and shoot her dead right there in the science fiction aisle. Instead, he held out his hand to her, the acorn pinched between thumb and forefinger.

"You found this," he said. His voice was soft as dead leaves whispering over cold pavement. "Thank you."

"It's cool, man," Cressida replied.

"No, no, *no*! Each "no" was harsher than the last. "*I owe you, now.*" In the warm, musty air of the library, the smell of peach cigarillos was stronger than it had been on the bus and layered over something dark and loamy, like wet soil or tree moss.

"Dude, it's just a fucking acorn," Cressida said. She wondered if helping a stranger on the bus had been a mistake. She would have to be careful when she left the library, or else end up like those unfortunate drifters that tarried too long at the home of Ray and Faye Copeland.

"So, what do you want?" He spat the words at her, then seemed to realize how he sounded and said, more slowly this time. *"What can I do for you?"*

Two teenagers standing in front of the graphic novels were staring at them with eyes round as dinner plates.

"I don't want anything," Cressida replied. She had only just noticed that there was a leaf, starting to wilt from the cold but still fiery red in the center, tangled in the man's hair.

"Nonsense," he said. "There must be something you want."

A million dollars. For my roommate to never come home again, or at least do the dishes once in a while. A car so I don't have to take the bus anymore...

Cressida thought all of those things and said none of them. What she did say was, "No, sorry. I really can't think of anything right now."

"Well," the man said. "I'll just make do until you think of something." A vulpine smile pulled at the corners of his mouth, forming his lips into a sharp, perfect V. He pulled a yellowed piece of paper from the chest pocket of his coat and slid it between the pages of Cressida's book. "Until next time."

The words cast a sort of spell over her, and it wasn't until the man snapped upright and disappeared around the corner that it broke. Cressida stood there for a moment longer, stunned, but when the shock had faded, she checked out the book and made her way home. It wasn't until later, reading by lamplight, that she found the piece of paper between pages 38 and 39. It was a business card, printed on ivory cardstock and embellished with gold leaf. It read, "1 wish. No refunds or exchanges."

***

Every Tuesday and Thursday, Cressida dropped $1.50 in the farebox to take the bus to her 7 p.m. night class. That Tuesday was no different, until it was. The professor was droning on about the Pre-Raphaelite art movement and, searching for a pen to take notes, Cressida reached into her coat. There was no pen, but she did find the $1.50 she'd dropped in the farebox.

***

Every Tuesday and Thursday, her money appeared back in her pocket. She paid again, as usual, with six quarters. Then, she tried paying with a dollar bill and *two* quarters. She even tried paying with thirty nickels. But all the money she dropped in the farebox appeared back in her pocket, exactly as it had been before. The nickels had been especially noticeable. The moment she dropped the last one in, her coat pocket grew heavy again.

One Thursday after class, she walked to QuikTrip and paid cash for a Cherry Coke. The money stayed in the till. The spell, for she was convinced the man from the bus had cast some sort of spell on her, only worked on the bus. Cressida huffed and walked home, drinking her Cherry Coke. If a stranger was going to ensorcell her, she thought, he could've at least been more generous about it.

***

When the man reappeared, Cressida was listening to an audiobook of *The Occultist's Handbook*. There was much talk of crystals, and tarot, and divination, but none of spells that only paid the bus fare. The book *had* mentioned that all magic had a cost. What was the cost of this spell, then? Perhaps for every cent she saved on bus fare, she lost a second of her own life. She was afraid, so when the man marched through the open doors of the bus and plopped down next to her, she ripped out her headphones and hissed, "*What did you do to me?!*"

"I paid your bus fare," he replied. *Neverwhere* was open in his lap and he appeared to be a little annoyed that she had interrupted him. "Are you ready to make your wish now?"

"What is this? Are you some sort of wizard or...*something?!*" She felt like a sputtering idiot, but she'd been replaying their first meeting in her head for weeks, and the question had been gnawing at her just as long.

"No," he said. "I'm not a wizard."

"A genie?"

"If I say yes, will you make your wish now?"

Cressida snorted. "Absolutely not. Do you think I'm an idiot? Whatever I wish for, you'll twist it around and everything will be worse than before."

He stared at her, aghast. "*I will not!*" he said. There was dirt on his coat and smeared on his chin, but it looked like he'd combed his hair.

"What if I don't want a wish? What if I just want you to go away?"

"I owe you a debt. If you make the damned wish, I'll happily never speak to you again."

"Is this still about the acorn?" Cressida groaned. "*Jesus Christ.*"

The man said nothing. The dingy bus lights cast strange shadows over his face, turning his eyes black as ink, that true black that isn't a color, but the absolute absence of light.

The bus went *buh-bum-buh-bum-buh-bum* as it passed over a rumble strip and exited the highway. The sound seemed to snap the man out of a trance, and his eyes returned to normal. "So, what's your wish?" he asked.

"Don't have one."

"There must be *something*."

"Oh, there are plenty of somethings, but I don't trust you to give them to me."

"Well," he answered. "We shall have to work on that."

***

After that, every Tuesday and Thursday, the man would join Cressida on the bus to and from her night class. It seemed he had convinced himself that if he could guess her dearest and most secret wish, she would make it and set him free. For her part, Cressida had begun to look forward to these conversations in a way that made her feel absurd.

The man always brought something with him. First it was pastries. Raspberry and cream cheese, topped with slivered, roasted almonds. As they ate, he asked, "Do you want to be rich?"

"Everyone wants to be rich," she'd said. But no, that was not her wish.

Next, he brought a kitten. It was tiny and black, with white socks on its two front paws. He had it cradled in the front of his coat and it was mewling pitifully.

"My apartment doesn't allow pets," Cressida said.

"Do you wish they did?" he asked, and they both laughed. She

67

took the cat home anyway and hid him in her bedroom and named him Acorn. The second time she heard the man laugh, it was because she'd just told him the kitten's name.

One night after class, she introduced him to *The NoSleep Podcast*. They listened to a story called *The Djinn Bottle*. It was about a man that purchased a magic bottle that could hold all of his weariness...at a cost.

"See?" Cressida told him, "That's the sort of thing that makes people not trust wishes."

"Let's listen to another one," he said.

After that, he brought bundles of wildflowers. Asters and blue thistle and bright yellow coneflowers.

"Did you pick these yourself?" Cressida asked.

"I grew them," he said. And that night he didn't ask for a wish.

***

The next Tuesday, the man wasn't on the bus. Then Thursday passed with no sign of him. Then another Tuesday, and another Thursday. On the fourth night without him, Cressida skipped class and rode the bus until the driver announced at 12:06 that they'd reached the last stop of the night. She was three miles from home, and she walked the whole way, trudging down the dimly lit sidewalks and feeling incredibly foolish.

There are two kinds of revelations: the slow, creeping ones that bubble up like water kept over low heat, and the sudden ones that crash into our lives like meteors or traffic accidents. Cressida's revelation was the latter, and it was this. She knew what to wish for.

***

The man reappeared on the last Thursday of Cressida's night class. Winter break would be starting soon, and she would have no reason to ride the bus, at least, not the same reason as before. But that didn't matter, did it? After all, the ride was free.

The first thing he said was, "I'm sorry."

"I thought you might have given my wish to someone else," Cressida joked.

It was quiet. There was no one else on the bus, and she was afraid that her heart was beating so loudly he might hear it thudding against her ribcage.

"I just needed to rest," he said, then added cryptically, gesturing around the bus cabin with a wide sweep of his hand, "There's iron under all this paint you know."

Cressida filed the comment away for later. She wouldn't, *couldn't* consider it too carefully now.

"I'm ready to make my wish." She blurted the words out, afraid that if she held them in a moment longer, she'd lose her nerve.

The man leaned forward in the bus seat, obscuring the view of the seat across the aisle. She had thought he'd be pleased, but his mouth was set in a grim line.

"What is it?"

"Can I tell you something first?"

"Of course," he said. He drummed his fingers on the seat in front of him. It was a very human gesture.

"My name. It's Cressida."

"Rowan," the man said, and smiled. *Rowan, Rowan.* She fought the urge to speak his name aloud. They would be at her stop soon.

"This is my last day of class," Cressida said. "I won't be riding the bus for a while."

"Oh," he said. "I suppose that's why you want to make your wish now."

"Yes...it is." She sucked in a breath of fetid bus air. She had always hated the bus, but now...she thought she might miss it.

"I wish...that I could see you again."

He said nothing, just stared at her with eyes dark and shining like slick pavement after a heavy rain.

"I mean," she went on, desperate to fill the silence, "There's not really a reason for us to see each other. I've had my wish. You don't owe me anymore and we probably won't meet on the bus again, so —"

He laughed then, and the sound was like the chiming of silver bells. "No," he said. "But a wish is a wish."

Accidental Kaiju

Dianne M. Williams

Dianne M. Williams is a writer of the speculative and weird from Lawrence, KS.

Grendela climbed the volcano in the early morning light of her thirteenth birthday. Thirteen was a magic age. At thirteen she would become a fully-fledged kaiju. Grendela: Destroyer of Cities. It was a great honor in her family. They had a nice little village all picked out for her to smash into the ground this morning. There would be a ceremony while the villagers fled for their lives. Her grandmother had probably made a cake. It was probably cooling right now, waiting to be frosted.

She wasn't going to destroy any villages today, though. Let them eat her cake without her; she didn't care. Her whole family were kaiju, dating back to the old days of the legendary monsters. But Grendela didn't want to be just one more giant monster. She wanted to be an environmental scientist.

She'd tried to explain it to her family for weeks. "You can't be a scientist. Look at you! You're a walking science experiment," her mother said.

Her father wasn't any more helpful. "You're a lava monster. You'll just have to learn how to deal with it. Learn to be the best lava monster you can be."

"When I was your age, I couldn't wait to collapse my first roof. That's the problem with kids these days. They all want to knock over a few landmarks here and there but none of them want to put in the work on the smaller villages. Don't want to work their way up anymore," her grandfather said. But Grandfather Kaiju said a lot of things that didn't seem to have anything to do with Grendela.

None of them understood her.

She dragged the equipment for her experiment behind her in a little red wagon the size of a human minivan. It bounced and clanged as she plodded up the mountainside, watching for loose dirt or particularly sharp boulders underfoot. Pine branches brushed her dark hide and pulled at the canvas bag in her wagon. She would show them.

Grendela was descended from a long line of lava monsters. It was in her blood. And in her feet. She could sense the magma trapped underground as she walked. Great pools and rivers of it. She looked for something with every step. She needed the perfect pool of lava to set up her experiment. Not too big and not under too much pressure. She followed a line of magma step by step up the mountain until she found it.

Her little red wagon squeaked as she dropped the handle. It was a simple experiment: a turbine sitting atop an aluminum tripod, a jug of water, and a little light board she'd built out of spare parts. The dirt was soft where she wanted to setup and the tripod settled at an odd angle once she got it situated, but it didn't take long. It took her longer to get her cellphone setup far enough back so that she could fit her entire kaiju body in the shot. She didn't get a lot of signal on the mountain, but hopefully it would be enough to live-stream her video.

The light of the camera gleamed off her teeth as she pulled her lips back in her best kaiju grin.

"Hi internet. You don't know me, yet, but you will soon. My name is Grendela and I want to show you how I, a kaiju, can give power to human cities," she said to the camera. "The only thing that keeps scientists from using volcanoes to power your cities is that it's so hard for humans to find safe, unpressurized pockets of magma. I can do it, though. And this is how I prove that I can do it."

She swept her arm out to show off her equipment.

"This is a very simple setup. I'm going to use my kaiju claws to drill down into the Earth. There's a nice little pocket of magma beneath me. I can sense it. Once I hit the magma, I'll pour water down into the hole. The water will turn to steam. The steam will rise to the surface and spin the blades on the turbine, powering the light board. When this light turns on, you'll know that I've succeeded."

She flexed her brown claws, each a foot long, to show her audience. And then she punched them into the soft earth, spinning them down, down, down. The hide on her hand soaked in the Earth's heat as gladly as she drilled deeper.

She stopped as the magma caught the tips of her claws. Snatching them back out of the hole, she blew on the ends to put the tiny flames out. She turned back to the camera and gave another, smaller grin.

"We've struck magma."

Next came the water. She struggled to get her arms wrapped around the jug she'd hauled up in her wagon. An awkward grip was all she could manage and she almost dropped it as she tipped the water out over the hole, releasing a steady trickle of water.

She stepped back to wait, her whole body tense muscle and

scales. The tips of her claws tasted like dirt and burning as she sucked at them. The steam should rise to the surface any minute now. Any minute and then the turbines would start to spin. It shouldn't take long.

She gave the camera another snouty grin, fully aware that the internet was watching her. Waiting with her. Judging her.

In her mind, she ticked off the number of things that could have gone wrong. Maybe she needed more water. Maybe there was too much room in the magma cavern and the steam wasn't going to come out. Maybe the magma or the dirt was just absorbing it.

"It should happen any moment." She tapped her claws against her snout. "The steam has a long way to travel, remember."

She could sense the magma just waiting for her, down there. There was no way she'd made a mistake about that. The whole day would be wasted if she had to go back and find more water to try again. She was a magma-sensing monster, not a diving rod.

She tapped her foot in irritation and the turbine jiggled on its soft base. The blades gave a half-hearted turn and then gave up before making even a full revolution. The light board didn't even flicker.

She was just about to pack up her wagon again when a puff of steam appeared at the top of the hole. Just a tiny little cloud, barely more than a whisper's breath. The little white puff didn't even reach her turbine's blades before it dissipated in the wind.

It wasn't enough. She'd have to come back with more water. She needed a fire hose up here given the weak little puff her huge jug of water produced. She had no idea how she could manage to drag enough water up here for her experiment. The sun was almost to the top of the sky already. It would be dark before she could do it.

She was trying to find a way to explain all of this to the internet when her feet felt something new. The ground beneath her shook. The magma beneath churned. And steam roared to the surface.

This time it was no wispy cloud but a geyser of steam. It blasted the turbine, spinning the metal blades and condensing back into water, only to drip back into the steam cloud and come back as fresh power. Grendela let out a whoop that shook birds from the trees down the mountain as the bulbs on her light board came on. Every single one of them. Her little turbine produced more power than she ever could have anticipated.

"You see that, internet! Do you see those beautiful little light bulbs? That's the power a kaiju like me could unlock for your cities. All of the power and more is waiting beneath the Earth just waiting to be tapped. And I'm coming to release it for you."

But something was wrong. She could feel it down to her magma-sensing bones. She'd felt it for minutes now. She was hoping that it would go away on its own, but it wasn't. It was getting worse. She was a lava monster. She wasn't wrong about these things.

The magma was rising to the surface.

Grendela scraped earth back over the hole with her claws, trying to seal it up. She looked around for particularly big rocks she could add to hold it all in place. But the magma beneath the surface was melting them, gobbling them up, as it climbed to the surface. It was too hot and under too much pressure.

The magma understood only two things: too little space and a hole that led out. The acrid smell of burning earth filled her snout. She had no choice but to back off. Her hide could take heat but she was pretty sure it couldn't withstand lava, yet. She backed into her cellphone and heard the sickening crunch of a screen cracking. That would put an end to her glorious live broadcast.

She watched as magma bubbled out of the ground. Great globs of it splattered out of the hole. Her turbine melted as the lava wrapped itself around the metal legs. The light board was next, collapsing like it was made of nothing more than butter.

The ground crackled and cracked open. Just little cracks at first, but they grew and spread. Grendela struggled to keep her balance as the ground became unstable beneath her. The Earth roared. It was no throaty rumble, but the thunderous sound of the Earth breaking from deep within. Each crack and crevice spat lava as the force of the magma ripped the crust apart.

"No, no, no, no," Grendela said as the cracks spread. "No, please stop."

She covered her ears against the noise, wrapping her claws around her head. The lava fountains sprouted every few feet, moving toward the village at the base of the mountain.

"Not the village," she said to the fissure she'd created. But it ignored her or couldn't hear her over the din.

Lava and the smell of scorched earth spread until it mixed with the local vegetation and became the smell and the smoke of trees burning. It stung Grendela's eyes.

She didn't know what to do. The village was in the path of both fire and lava. Human villages seemed so very flammable.

She turned and ran down the hillside, clawed hands splayed out behind her. This time she didn't watch for such minor things as tree branches. Sap clung to her legs as she pushed her way through the forest.

The village was an old one. The buildings were made of the gray mountain stone. People formed lines between the water tower and the homes closest to the spreading fire. They used fire hoses, garden hoses, and passed buckets from hand to hand, dousing shingled roofs and wooden fences. They could see the black smoke rising from the trees, but hadn't yet realized the full danger. They couldn't see the lava bearing down on them.

Grendela knocked over a withered old pine as she burst out of the trees. Black smoke billowed around her as the wind pushed the fire closer to the village. The first villagers to notice her dropped their buckets and screamed. One-by-one the rest looked up. Their eyes widened in fear. They dropped what they were holding. The last remaining patches of dry ground turned to mud as hoses were left forgotten. A couple of them pulled out cell phones to snap pictures of her.

"What are you all still doing here? You can't be here," she roared. It came out sounding much harsher than she meant.

The small people beneath her flailed. Cars started all over the village. Some of them threw things at her. Buckets and garden tools bounced and crashed against the tough hide of her shins.

"Hey, cut it out," she said. "I'm trying to help you."

Grendela lumbered into the village. Each footstep shook items loose from the human houses. Wind chimes crashed. Windows shattered. Precious and fragile things were crushed by her careless steps.

A little girl running across her path slipped in the mud and landed hard on her butt. Her powder blue shirt was soaked through. Mud packed her hair to her shoulders. Grendela reached one clawed hand down to help her up, and the child wailed. Grendela jumped back. Her elbow caught the water tower and knocked it over. Water washed out gardens and swept the little girl even further from Grendela as it raced across the open space of the village. The girl's mother scooped her up and they got into a car and sped away, fishtailing in the mud.

"Sorry," Grendela called after them as they went. The last few people fled and she was left standing alone among the empty homes. Flames leapt from rooftop to rooftop as if avoiding the lava that hadn't yet reached the village floor. The smoke rose up into her face and coated the insides of her nostrils. She was never going to get rid of that smell.

She tried to put out the fire on the nearest roof. She swatted at the flames with her hands, but the structural supports of the home were weakened by fire and the whole house collapsed. The fire latched onto anything inside that it could consume. Carpets, beams, mementos. The fire didn't care.

There were no hoses left. No rains coming. The sky, what Grendela could see of it through the smoke, was clear and blue. There was nothing she could do. She wandered back into the forest, but couldn't bring herself to look away. From the trees, she watched the buildings burn to the ground, wiping her eyes with sooty hands.

Lava joined the flames slowly, seeping into the village. It crackled and steamed as the mud tried to cool it, but the lava marched on. Within hours it had covered or consumed everything it touched, taking back the mountain stones that had been buildings only that morning.

***

There was a huge "CONGRATULATIONS" banner hanging over the doorway when she got home. Its red letters mocked her. She wiped her feet on the mat, leaving it black with soot. More soot smeared the brass door handle as she let herself in, trying to wipe her face clean with her other arm.

The living room was crowded with giant monsters. A newscaster's voice narrated the destruction of a local village by a new kaiju. Grendela's name wasn't mentioned, but she knew her picture with black smoke and flames behind her would be on every station tonight.

Her mother wrapped blue tentacles around Grendela, twining them all the way down to the claws she trapped at Grendela's sides.

"Oh darling, are you okay? We saw your live broadcast and then watched the rest on the news. What an amazing way to destroy your first village! And we thought this environmental science stuff wouldn't amount to anything," her mother said.

"Um, mom that's not really what I was-" Grendela started.

But her father was slapping her on the back with his own claws. "It's in the blood," he said. "You'll make a fine lava monster."

Grendela sighed, waiting for her mother to disengage her tentacles so that she could wipe the tears from her eyes.

"I broke my phone," she said. They all seemed to ignore the way her voice cracked.

"Well that's one of the hazards of being a kaiju!" her father said. "We'll get you a new one with a better case. You've earned it. Now come in and have some cake."

The cake was a tall chocolate cake, ringed with plastic green trees. A strawberry filling oozed out of the top. Some of it was plopped on top of several haystack cookie huts scattered around the base. Grendela turned away.

"I really should clean up," she said.

"Nonsense! We're all kaiju here," her father said. "We're used to a little dirt and smoke."

He took her by the shoulders and guided her forward as the rest of the family stood to congratulate her. Tentacles and claws were everywhere.

From the dining room, her grandmother beckoned to her with one withered, old tentacle, drawing her off from the crowd while the cake was being handed around.

Grendela slumped her shoulders and followed. At least the other room was quieter.

"I thought it was a nice experiment, dear," she said, handing Grendela a neatly wrapped package. "I think you have a lot to offer science, even if they don't know it yet."

The paper was decorated with microscopes and atomic symbols. Grandela pulled gently at a ribbon the color of lava, careful not to destroy the present within.

As she pulled the paper off with her claws, she laughed and hugged her grandmother, crushing her poor shoulders as tears stung her eyes. Inside was a thick textbook. The cover showed a color image of one of her ancestors with hot magma pouring from a volcano behind him. *Kaiju and the Environment: How Giant Monsters Change Our Planet*.

"There's a chapter in there about volcanoes and geothermal power," her grandmother said as Grendela flipped through the pages.

"Thank you. I can't wait to read it."

Her grandmother understood.

First appeared at *The Confabulator Cafe*, July 2016

The Glitch

Aimée Jodoin

Aimée Jodoin has a degree in English and lives in Michigan. She reads books for a living as a librarian and freelance reviewer, and she writes speculative fiction in her spare time. She is passionate about environmentalism, health, and cats.

Glitches don't happen nearly enough.

Usually it's not so bad. An arm here. A foot there. Injuries easy to forgive but flaws hard for Rehabilitation to admit. They sweep it under the rug. Pull the traveler from the program. Tell the public it's too many travelers in the system, too many for the program to handle, and claim the injury is justice for the remaining time owed Rehabilitation for their crime. The traveler's sentence is up, and they get to go home.

Occasionally, glitches can be gruesome. A head. A slice through the torso. Skin turned inside out. Disappearance from existence altogether. To the public, irreconcilable behavior on the other side, Rehabilitation claims.

It's a risk, Michael tells me, he's willing to take.

I'm a technician. Most of my job is pulling the lever. But if there's a problem—a glitch, a processing error, a weird noise—I get to open up the machine and look for the piston that misfired, the wiring that's loose, the piece that's jammed. I report the problem and fix it before it can cause something more serious.

But like I said, glitches are rare, the opportunities for sabotage minuscule. So Michael remains imprisoned, and I continue to spend my nights alone.

Much of my life before his sentencing contained the warmth of his body against mine in bed—shifts for technicians at Rehabilitation are too long to allow for many daytime activities during the week—and weekends walking the public museums and parks, Saturday nights playing sloppy-drunk pool with friends at the pub down the street.

Now my weekends are empty. Feet propped up on the coffee table. Beer in hand. Chinese takeout growing cold next to me. Old documentaries streaming on the television in perpetuity. Can't go out with my friends without Michael. That feels like betrayal.

My dreams are filled with Michael and the lever.

That lever is the focus of my attention the majority of my days. Six hours pulling every fifteen seconds. A two hour break on which the day hinges, in which I can eat some lunch or, before his crime, rush home for a quickie with Michael. Six hours pushing every fifteen seconds. From 6am to 8pm every weekday, Rehabilitation rules my life.

A few years ago, I would have thought this job was made-up. Now it's like I've been doing it forever. Every fifteen seconds in the morning, I pull the lever to send a traveler sixty years in the future. Every fifteen seconds in the afternoon, I push the lever to receive them back in the present. 1440 travelers I'm responsible for.

One of them is Michael.

Rehabilitation calls them travelers instead of prisoners, which is really what they are. They've been convicted of crimes—some more serious than others—and sentenced to however many years of Rehabilitation the judicial system sees fit. Five days a week for eight-hour shifts of hard labor sixty years in the future. Fewer hours than me. Much, much fewer. But I'd rather pull the lever than do what they do.

When Michael was caught, his lawyers told him not to say anything, so he didn't. But at the courthouse, when I met with him privately before the trial, he told me the truth.

"I did it, you know," he said. No flicker of regret crossed his gaze.

"I know," I said. I didn't care what he had done. Don't care. He's my husband.

They could have assigned him to someone else. There are twenty-four technicians at the Chicago Rehabilitation location. I know it's random, but it feels like they assigned him to me as some sort of sick joke. Every weekday, I send him future-side at 10:13:15 am and pull him back at 6:13:15 pm. I see him for those brief moments, see his expression blank until he looks at me—then there's only sadness in his eyes—and try to send him messages from my mind to his.

I love you.

Be safe. Don't push yourself too hard. Don't let yourself stand out too much.

I'm working on it. It'll be soon.

But he never hears me, of course. His sad expression stays the same.

Visitation is once a week—Saturdays—for an hour. I go every time. That sad look is still there. He doesn't say much, and I don't blame him. I say a lot, and he probably wishes I wouldn't. Though if it were me, I would want to hear his voice as much as I could. It would remind me that there's still something good out there waiting for me. That there's more to life than sleeping, eating, and working future-side. That there's more to life than Rehabilitation.

To be honest, it would be nice to have that reminder now. When you're wrapped up in Rehabilitation—and you have no husband or friends or hobbies or life—it's all-consuming. All I think about is pulling the lever, pushing the lever, sending travelers future-side and pulling them back to the present. About what their work is like on the other side. About how hard it is and how easy I have it compared to them and how what we're doing is fulfilling a destiny we know we have already fulfilled and how if we stop, there's no telling what would happen.

Underpopulation is their problem, future-side; diminishing resources is ours, now. That's the deal. They send us power created from their limitless, sustainable technology; we send them manual labor. Why not just send us the energy with nothing in exchange, knowing their future depends on it? Because, then what's in it for them? They are human after all.

For the past fifty years, we knew there was a problem. But people continued to drive low-gas-mileage cars, to produce and consume items with plastic packaging, to leave their lights on for hours on end, to eat cows and drink milk and spray crops with pesticides. To reproduce and reproduce without doing anything to diminish the impact of their reproduction. Fossil fuel corporations continued to petition against regulations and to pay out the ass to stay obscenely rich. State governments continued to give less than two shits about infrastructure and water quality and air quality and trees. High-carbon-footprint buildings continued to be built. Carbon-removing forests continued to be chopped down. People pretended they cared. Governments pretended they cared. But the few people and governments who tried to do something were only met with more people, more demand, more chaos.

Hence, Rehabilitation.

When the United States government was contacted by some representatives of a mysterious corporation from sixty years in the future, it was a fucked-up science-fiction dream come true.

Apparently, we will continue to drive cars and buy plastic and leave our lights on and eat cows for the next fifty years. People will die. Lots of people. Tsunamis, droughts, famines, hurricanes, genocides—you name it. We will continue to fuck up until we run out of both fuel and people, and until the idea of time-imported slaves becomes an idea we can get behind.

So here I am, fulfilling my destiny.

With Michael, I didn't think about what I was doing too much. I pulled the lever. I pushed the lever. I came home to Michael. Not like it's the most glamorous job. I had some reservations at first, thinking, Do I really want to be part of this system? Culpable for perpetuating a business that has kept certain groups of people oppressed for centuries? That saw my grandfather locked up for three years for a crime he didn't commit? That involved strange technology and strange people we didn't know we could trust?

But the alternative, was my thought process in accepting the position, is a future so bleak I won't want to be in it. That or someone else pulls the lever and gets the health insurance.

This was before Michael's sentencing. And well before he told me what was really happening on the other side.

When he told me, four visitations ago, that the future side was cheating, manipulating their more advanced technology to keep travelers several days at a time but making sure they still arrive on schedule daily our time, I was enraged. I wanted to report it to Rehabilitation immediately. But when he shook his head, dejected, I knew it would do no good. They might already be aware of the situation. Could be in on it, getting more, unreported energy in exchange for the secret extended sentences. Travelers are tools to them. No longer human beings once they've been sentenced.

They hide the glitches from the public. Of course they would be hiding other things.

It's been eight weeks since our last glitch. A man came through with only half a body. Or rather, only half his body came through. The other half was left behind, sixty years from now, where the Rehabilitation staff likely gawked madly, just as they do present-side when something like that happens. We got his front half. A face so sad and exhausted, unaware of what had just happened to him it happened so fast. The shirtfront with his number stamped on it: Traveler 345682. The toe-end of his shoes, holding onto his ankles by hardly an inch of flesh. His back half we would never see. He'd be buried in two different times. Or burned. Let's not kid ourselves; they don't give glitched travelers an honorable funeral. They pretend that shit never happened, like farts in a nursing home.

The glitch didn't happen on my machine. It was the technician next to me who had to deal with the consequences. A thorough search of the machine to find the wrecked part. Lots of paperwork. Staying late to make sure all the other travelers assigned to her made it through. I am not envious. I've been there myself.

And today, I'll be there again.

It has to be today. There was a glitch on my machine. A man came through without his left hand. Spurting blood. Howling in pain. He grasped at it, the place where his hand had been a moment ago, and he fell to his knees as the blood poured through the fingers of his right hand.

A nice little severance for him.

Vi is next to me in a flash. As shift manager, she's always on top of her game.

"Open 'er up," she says. Medics rush to the injured traveler's side.

I pop open the panel on the back of the machine and reach my hand inside. I feel around. There's a cable that's come undone. It's shimmied out of its plug.

"Left stabilizer uncorked," I say. A glitch that has happened before on other machines, but not mine. A simple one, for both the technician and the traveler. We should both count ourselves lucky.

I grab the cable and slide it back into the plug, but I don't slide it in all the way. In an hour or two, by the time it's Michael's turn to be pulled through, it will have shimmied out again.

Glitches are rare. To have two glitches in one day is unheard of. I'm risking getting caught. But it's a risk I'm willing to take to get my husband back.

Vi takes a flashlight to the panel once I step away, double-checking my work. The shine reflects off the metal and back at me. She sees the cord that had come loose. She touches the base of the plug. She steps away and clicks off the flashlight.

"Alright. Close 'er up. Have your report to me by tomorrow morning."

I nod. I'll write the report tonight, the nod says. And hopefully another report, too, with Michael's name at the top of it. She didn't see that the plug was still a little loose. She didn't see my sabotage.

The medics get the traveler out of the frame in less than two minutes, just barely delaying the schedule. That's how they do it. Get the traveler out of the way as soon as possible. Before the next one is sent through. It was only a hand. They'll have it cleaned up future-side in no time.

It's another thirty seconds after he's away that my machine flashes the number of the next traveler. I push the lever.

I push the lever.

I push the lever.

I push the lever.

I push the lever.

An hour of pushing the lever goes by. Usually I would lose track of time. But my heart is in my throat. Sweat beads down my temple. I feel the gravity of every push of the lever. This could be the one. This next one could be the glitch. Hold out, hold out. Just another thirty-four pushes. Just another twenty.

Buzz. Hiss. Traveler steps away. Buzz. Hiss. She steps aside. Buzz. Hiss. A guard yanks him out of the frame. Buzz. Hiss.

Traveler 142648 incoming displays on the screen. Finally, finally. A number I've memorized. A number that dances across my dreams.

I push the lever.

There's the usual buzz, then a clunk. The zap as Michael is sent through.

"Shit," Vi says after a beat. "Got another one."

Moonlight Plastics

Rachel Brittain

Rachel Brittain is a writer from Arkansas. When she isn't writing books, she's writing about books for Book Riot. Her fiction has appeared in Andromeda Spaceways, The Conium Review, as the title story in in My Name Was Never Frankenstein and elsewhere.

Garbage, microscopic plastic particles of it, rushed up her nose, stinging. Her lungs burned to cough. Sana was drowning, though that was the least of her problems.

She'd botched the job—bad—and somehow let the mark get away—worse—so even bleeding out five feet under paled in comparison. She'd expected the rough waters, expected the scrappers to fight back, but the moment the gun had been pulled there was just a split second of the hesitation she'd thought had been trained out of her, and that was all it took. Point-blank, shot by her own mark. The shame was enough to kill her if the internal bleeding didn't do the job first.

It shouldn't have slowed her down. Pain was trained out of her too—meant to be, anyway. There would be much worse than a bullet wound waiting for her on the other side of this, assuming she didn't die first. But it didn't so much matter now, did it? She was already dying, and she'd lost her speeder too—which shouldn't rank, but only because she was being grit-toothed practical about it. She really loved that speeder.

Moonlight, golden white, refracted through the surface of the water, drifting slowly away as she sank deeper. There was a tendril of blood trailing back to the surface. Drowning, bleeding out, she was a dead woman anyway. Might as well enjoy the dancing play of light filtering down through shifting fragments of garbage.

A hand reaching out...

Sana was drowning.

And then she wasn't.

***

A simple job. But they were always supposed to be simple, weren't they? Just make the mark. Not even a catch and return, not even a kill job. All she had to do was tag them so the company could keep tabs, so they couldn't pick their nose or scratch their ass without someone knowing about it. That simple.

But all it took was one miscalculation, one reflexive flinch before instinct could kick in, one stupid little mistake, and a simple job became your last job. Sana knew that. But then, everyone's invincible until they aren't, right? That's human nature.

The waves in the middle of the Pacific were like concrete walls of water, rising and falling and shifting the ground beneath, forever reorienting perspective. There was no reprieve, no moment of rest or respite—too long a blink and you might find yourself coughing up a lungful of water.

She pulled her goggles down and readjusted the thin, black breathing mask fitted over her mouth and nose—the only thing standing between her and so much toxic air. The fumes floating up from the garbage gyre stung the exposed skin at the edges of her mask. The sun baked the chemicals right out of them, all those plastic particulates pulled here by the currents. Most of it dumped in the twenty-cen. Ancient fuckers didn't even care what they were flushing down the drain: a legacy of garbage decaying out here in the deep for their great-great-to-the-power-of-great grandkids to choke on.

She was gaining on them, her speeder skimming over the water and kicking up a salty spray. Just aim the tracker gun, burn a little laser barcode into their skin from fifty yards. Easy. Until a piece of plastic flew up, nicking her goggles, half-blinding her. Until one of them pulled a gun—an ancient thing which shouldn't have worked, much less from this distance. Must've been jacked, teched-up somehow.

Until they pulled the trigger and she felt the sucker-punch impact that knocked her off balance. Until her immortal number was up and she was drowning in plastic, and, well, you get the picture: bad and bad. Fatally bad.

She scrambled against the running board of the speeder, the harsh downdraft tossing her out across the water, splayed and grasping, and then under, buffeted deep, waves breaking below her feet overhead. Torqued over. Water gushing through the filter of her mask, pushing at the back of her throat.

What a stupid fucking useless way to go.

***

Sana had taken a blow to the head. Subdermal hematoma, maybe. Flat-out lost it, at any rate. That much was evident, the only explanation, the only thing that made any sense as to why a mermaid—a kripping gorgeous mermaid with a salt-tarnished, metal tail—was dragging her to safety from the whirl of the Great Pacific Garbage Gyre.

Except, maybe not saving. Because down was up and sunlight was below and that hand was dragging her away which meant she was being dragged *down*. Deeper and deeper, pressure building.

Less of a mermaid, more of a siren, then. But what did fictional semantics matter? She could worry about words and the many mistakes that led to them—the choice of her unstable old, speeder and a hot meal over the credits for a safer, newer option; the way she'd shifted at the last second so the bullet hit her dead on instead of clipping her at an angle; the fact she'd taken this job in the first place because it was the most isolated, most exciting, and yet not even the biggest payout—or just accept that she was being dragged to her death.

Well, Sana could think of worse ways to die than in the arms of a beautiful siren.

(Drowning wasn't so bad, as far as these things went. Relatively peaceful once you accepted it for what it was. Stop panicking and just breathe, natural, let the water flow in and take you. No drawn-out, painful struggle. No questions or accusations. Just inevitability.)

Pleasantly numb and floaty—Sana was content to drift into unawareness.

But—and she noted this with some concern, because this was something else, some unaccounted-for alternative—she didn't seem to be dying. Her head was clearing, images coming into better focus even as the water around them continued to warp her perception. That's when she realized there was a rebreather in her mouth.

Sana sucked in a greedy breath. Sweet, sweet, recycled oxygen—because god-kripping-damn-it this was definitely the unaccounted-for something else—and finally, gladly, passed out.

***

Lying on the floor—metal or something like it. Metal alloy. Expensive. She could hear movement across from her, shifting, scuttling. Her captor. Sana cracked her eyelids, crusty with saltwater, just enough to see without being seen.

The mermaid was detaching her tail.

No. Sana blinked. Her mind was still connecting incoherent thoughts. The woman—because she was certainly a human woman—was removing some sort of fin attached at the knees. She set it aside, hanging from a hook on the wall where a steady patter of droplets fell from segmented tailfins.

The woman pulled out a pair of curved, walking blades, and it was clear now that the fin Sana's hypoxiated brain had mistaken for a mermaid tail was just a prosthetic. No mythical creature, but a feat of engineering. Clever.

Too bad, really. All things considered, she would've preferred a touch of fantasy.

Sana felt the familiar press of dense polymer at her lower back. The woman hadn't searched her, hadn't even restrained her. Not so clever then.

She reached for the gun holstered just beneath the soaked hem of her shirt, shoulders and chest protesting the movement. Injured, but that was a problem for later. This gun was real, not the laser tagger lost back with her speeder. Plastic-polymer with biodegradable bullets—unlike the one that had passed clear through her shoulder.

Teeth gritted. Carefully, without betraying anything but the slightest movement, she freed the weapon and took aim.

The woman was gone. Sana barely had time to track movement to her right—the woman was behind her, how, and so quickly?—when she felt a sharp prick at the base of her neck—kripping hell—and drifted back into black.

***

One of her wrists was cuffed to the water line, a thin film of condensation clinging to the metal. A steady drip-drip-drip of water fell against her wrist, dragging a line of cold down her arm. She tugged halfheartedly, already knowing it would be sound. More "rote motion" than "escape attempt".

Her other wrist was free—which might've been a rookie mistake, except the woman had learned from last time. Gun missing, and she'd clearly been searched. Thoroughly. No tasers or knives, and the hidden blade compartments lining the seams of her clothes would be useless considering she wasn't currently wearing them.

Stripped down to her skivvies, clothes hung to dry haphazardly around the room. On the back of the chair; hanging off hooks. Her leather jacket was draped over a pipe near the ceiling. A snailtrail of water dripped down its sleeve, sluggishly. Sana shuddered. It was real leather—grown in a lab, worth more than both her kidneys on the black market. She'd kill for that thing; loved it more than her own mother.

She pushed herself up to sitting and scanned the room. Stereotypical lab equipment: vials of rose- and teal-colored luminescent fluids and jars of indiscernible specimens. A work table under the port window covered in mess. Half-eaten protein packet, spilled caf mug, scattered papers. But the vials themselves were meticulously labeled—careless only where it didn't count.

She stretched to peer into the rest of the space—small and damp, but sturdy; made to stand up to immense deep-sea pressures, which made her think of some sort of submersible lair—but a sharp, tugging pain followed by a deep ache stopped her. Injured, right.

Unclothed as she was, a simple glance down was enough to tell her that her wounds had been tended. Her fingers traced butterfly stitches which pulled the edges of the gash on her forehead together. Old fashioned, gauze bandages wrapped her upper arm and shoulder.

She peeled back the edge to bruised and tender flesh underneath. The stitches were crude, but even. Passable. She'd certainly done worse herself.

It would scar, no question, but Sana didn't mind. Scars were a commodity in her line of work, better than any résumé or recommendation. Flesh ripped open and sewn back together, puckered and red and grisly—there was something striking about that. It meant your survival was hard fought. Proof of life.

And the black silk sutures themselves—not surprising there'd be no medical adhesive in a place like this. Sana lived hard, but even her cityrat life was a step above this middle of nowhere scrapper. Honest, who made a home in the middle of the Pacific? Flat-out mad people was who.

Said madwoman walked back into the room, hips swinging out to accommodate the blades she walked on. She didn't acknowledge her—sitting up and fully conscious, mostly unclothed—which disconcerted Sana, who'd expected at least a *good you're awake* or a *not so quick with your gun this time, I see*. Instead she just checked the cuff holding Sana's wrist and glanced at the exposed stitching beneath her collarbone then went on like she had better things to do. More important than a naked prisoner strapped to her waterline.

Cuffed and gunless, Sana had no idea how to properly handle this situation. Violence, maybe. Except being stripped and strung-up made that a bit trickier, didn't it? And she'd already made the mistake of underestimating this woman once.

"I'm your prisoner now, is that it?" Sana called out. The woman ignored her, out of sheer spite, Sana felt certain. She went back to her bench. Examined some instruments and scribbled notes longhand in the open notebook like she was living in the twenty-first century.

"Why'd you bring me here anyway?" Silence. She moved through corners of the room, to places Sana's eyes couldn't follow. The torque against the arm cuffed over her head would've snapped her wrist—though she did pull at it just to try, or maybe because the sharp lightning tug of pain jolted through her brain like caffeine.

Sana gritted her teeth. "Not that I'm not enjoying this, but if you're determined to ignore me, why not just let me go?"

"Your presence could skew the results," she said finally, the other woman.

Not an accent she recognized. Not American Provinces or the Great Northern Conglomerate and not the Allied Arab Nations where Sana had grown up—what growing up there had been to do, anyway. An indiscernible accent couldn't tell much except that she'd probably been rich enough and educated enough to lose whatever accent she'd had in the first place. There was power in anonymity.

Sana let that hang in the air. "Your…results?"

The woman didn't turn around. "Yes."

"So I'm your prisoner."

"Only until the experiment's finished." The woman walked out of the shadows, pulling off latex gloves, rolled inside-out and left on the table. Still some bloody gauze up there, too, now, Sana noticed.

She made no attempts to cover herself despite her not-insubstantial state of undress. If the madwoman hadn't wanted to see her half-naked she shouldn't have cuffed and stripped her. Not to mention, she must've seen a good portion of what there was to be seen when she'd tended to Sana wounds in the first place.

The woman was smart, well-trained. Said only what she needed to say and no more. She had a pair of vintage glasses pushed up on her forehead—which said something about her person, that she'd opt for the outmoded frames instead of implants or augs. Some weird psychology there.

Madwoman noticed her staring; raised a pointed eyebrow.

"Hey, I'm not the one bringing strange women back to my underwater lair and drugging them up, stripped and handcuffed to the wall," Sana said—before adding with a coy, dangerous edge, "not that I might not be into that, right circumstances and all."

She didn't take the bait—but then where was the fun in easy prey?

"Maybe you could find out if you let me loose."

No shift in the other woman's expression until Sana tugged meaningfully at her cuffed wrist. Gentle lines tightened around the madwoman's eyes, the only sign of her comprehension.

"I saved your life," she said, looking pointedly at the bandages taped across Sana's torso. "You're welcome for that."

Which apparently settled it.

***

Later, Sana realized the question she should've asked was how long, exactly, this experiment was going to last. Not why or what—though she suspected the madwoman would've loved to explain the whys and whats in excruciating detail, scientists always did—but just how long exactly, because it had been however many hours now and Sana was beginning to realize that in addition to the blood loss and the head injury and the near-drowning, it'd been quite a while since she'd had anything more than polluted sea water in her system.

Not a winning combination, according to the headache beating against the inside of her skull.

But the woman didn't like to answer questions, however she phrased them. "How long are you going to keep me here?" Silence. "Experiment, huh?" Silence. "Maybe uncuff me or give me some kripping water already!" A glass of water slid her way, sloshing over the sides and adding to the slick dampness of the floor. She stretched awkwardly to reach, one arm still shackled overhead.

"What's your name, anyway?" Sana asked after taking a sip, speaking only to fill the silence. The depth of it, unsettling.

But the woman responded without looking back. "So you can report it back to those corps you work for?" She said it, not accusatory, but plainspoken in the way of everything else. Matter-of-fact.

It took Sana longer to answer than it should've. "I don't work for anybody," she said. More guile than Sana had pegged her for, though, which was interesting in its own right.

"Who pays for all the scrap you drag in then? Who pays out the bounties you don't lose in the middle of the ocean?"

Much more guile. Maybe Sana should've known better than to think a scientist clever enough to survive out here would be any kind of simple. An interesting knot to untangle, if she could just free up her hands long enough pull at it.

"What's your name?" Sana asked again to no answer. "My name's Sana."

"I know."

Sana narrowed her eyes at that. Annoying and likely untrue. Her files were all redacted, street cam footage erased, no trails for any other companies to track or—

The woman pulled out the identification stick that had been tucked beneath Sana's shirt before the accident and was, of course, missing along with the rest of her clothes. Sana gritted her teeth. The woman must've done a hack job. So her knowledge of Sana's life was less guesswork and more identity theft.

A name didn't have any more power than you gave it, but that didn't mean you had to part with it easily. Especially when parting with it made you an identifiable target.

"You make a habit of ID theft with all your prisoners? This your way of getting to know us? Because, darling," she slipped into a sultry drawl, "you could've just asked."

"You're my first."

Her frank speech once again left Sana blinking to catch up. "I'm your—"

"Prisoner," she said. "You can call me Em."

"That your name?"

Em tossed her ID stick, Sana catching it between the edges of her fingertips even with one wrist cuffed. A glance up and down. Testing her reflexes, sizing her up, injuries and all. Em smiled and walked out, leaving her alone once again. Sana cocked her jaw in a thoughtfully pleased expression that sent aching tendrils up toward her temples. This, Sana could work with—and maybe even enjoy.

***

Sana dozed, restless. The woman—Em—came and went. Slipping on the fishtail and out of her blades, dripping a trail of saltwater as she settled on her bench, pipetting samples and adding in chemicals that shifted them every shade of green and pink and blue.

Sometimes, after hours and hours of fiddling with those samples, she'd open a panel that pulled out from the wall like a drawer, letting in a clear tank of ocean water she could partition off, sometimes with a few fish or plankton or—once—a jellyfish in with it. Once it was sealed, she'd carefully dropper in her colored solutions, now the pink, then the green. She'd watch, take careful measurements. The water and fish were always disposed of, never re-released.

"What is that? You a poisoner-chemist? Poisoning fish?" Nothing, and half the time Sana felt like she was talking just for the talking of it. Just because solitary was worse, and even though this wasn't solitary, the quiet was bad enough even when

Em was there. "Thought we had enough of that already. Fish is expensive enough, and here you are trying to poison off the rest of them."

The hum and creak of the pressure against the walls was the only response. Then: "Those corps you work for—" She shot Sana a pointed look as she pipetted. "—what is it you do for them—aside from drowning?"

"Couldn't piece it together from this then?" Sana waved her ID stick through the air, Em's eyes tracking the movement. "You didn't tell me yours, why should I tell you mine?"

The other woman shrugged, meaning to convey indifference. A bargaining chip, perhaps, if a small one. Her eyes darted up to the jacket slung over the pipe.

"Give me my leather, I'll tell you what it is you want to know."

Em eyed her, narrow and gauging. The thoughts flitted across her face and she did nothing to hide them—no proper training how to, maybe. *Why that? Why not freedom or painkillers? Is it valuable? Sentimental? Useful to my advantage?*

Cunning and secretive, but not wily, which might've been surprising—except maybe rich scientists who spent all their time doing experiments out in the middle of the ocean like old British spy movie villains didn't need much beyond that to get what they wanted. Maybe they could just buy it.

"Just the jacket," Sana said, answering the questions Em hadn't meant to ask.

She grabbed it—roughly— tossing it down, and Sana had to conceal the wince to catch it, the movement pulling at her shoulder. Not as if she could put it on, so she just held it in her hands. Should've made her more suspicious, that. The jacket had sentimental value, sure, and monetary, too, which was just as important, but why would Sana want it back when she couldn't even wear it? Why waste a bargain on nothing? That's what the woman should've been asking.

Instead, there was something like guilt in her eyes.

Sana could use that. The scientist hadn't realized yet what she'd done—rescued a cetacean only to tie up a feral shark, and Sana had fangs. Was made to *bite*.

"Your job, anyway," she said.

Sana considered toying with her, withholding just to see how she'd react—*reason? lash out? reverse transaction?*—but decided against it, mostly because she was too tired to reckon with any of that, however edifying.

"I'm the delivery girl," she said, shifting to rest against the wall as best she could. "I find whatever it is they're looking for; deliver it back to them."

Em eyed her. "That's not what your stick said."

Sana knew exactly what her stick said—and what it didn't. "You're a bad liar," she told her.

"So are you," Em said. "Unless you really expect me to believe a scrapper would risk their skin for some degrading plastic out here in the middle of the Pacific."

Sana shrugged. "Things are rough out there."

"Not that rough," she said. Then: "You're a bounty hunter." And if she'd known all this time, she might as well have come out and said it.

Sana bared her teeth in a smile—predatory, she'd been told. "That's right," she said, leaning forward, as much as the cuff and her protesting wounds would let her. "Are you so sure I'm not here to hunt you?"

***

The last hours had been wiled counting the passing schools of fish. Maybe not more than one at all, but a single school swimming round and round the Gyre indefinitely and forever.

Then again, maybe that was Sana's own nihilism speaking, stuck in a cage she might never find a way out of. Better would've been to count the days, tally the marks on the wall. A useful course of passing time. Not much point, though. Aside from the floodlights occasionally switched on around the submersible lab, sunlight didn't filter down this far. No way to track days and nights, just indeterminable periods of sleeping and waking until there didn't seem to be a point in asking what time it was or what day.

Em came and went, sometimes bringing food, between experiments, but largely ignored her beyond that. Finally, on the third day or the fifth day or maybe something more than that, Sana realized why.

"You don't like me," she said, when Em came out for the first daily check of her specimens. "Why?"

Em turned to face her, head cocked to one side as if she'd finally asked a mildly interesting question. "I don't think much about you at all."

Some people might've flinched at the honesty of it. Not Sana.

"But what you do think, you don't like," Sana persisted. "You don't know me—only read an ident stick. That's just words."

"I do actually," she said. "Know you. I know you like I know everyone, because you *are* everyone—living day to day, ignoring the world to make life better for yourself even with the air burning and the oceans rising around you. Selfish."

"And you're so much better? Out here on your own, ignoring the rest of us. I got plenty of problems all my own to deal with, alright?" said Sana.

"They're all our problems," said Em. "We all die if we don't fix them."

"Then we die!" said Sana. "You want to call me selfish? Everyone is selfish. The world is selfish—I'm not the one who made it this way."

"But you don't do anything to change it, do you?"

Sana scoffed. They were only going around in circles like everything else out here, circling the Gyre, and what was the point? "Think you're so smart, don't you?"

Em tipped her head. "A genius, actually."

She slid a plate across the floor, then, something fresh that smelled of roasting. It pulled a groan from Sana's stomach as she picked at the lump of whitish meat. "What is this?"

"Fish," said Em. "Halibut." Sana poked at it, picking off a flakey piece of flesh still attached to bone. Em watched the careful dissection. "It's not poisoned."

"Not one of your experiments?"

Em's lips twitched up into something that was almost a smile as she shook her head. "Fresh."

That was all Sana needed to raise the plate up to her mouth, using her knee for balance and her free hand to shovel the fish into her mouth—salty and sweet. So tender. She'd never had fish before—never been able to afford it—so had no way of knowing if this one was unusually good or just a sampling of the rest that was out there.

"Five percent, that's how much of our oceans have been explored," Em said as Sana ate, the scientist in her finally winning out into a lecture. "Only five percent. And thousands of marine species endangered—did you know that? Hundreds already lost. Some we never even knew."

Sana wasn't sure if she was meant to feel sorry for a bunch of fish—she mostly just wanted to know where she could get more of this one, the taste of it still melting into her mouth even as her tongue chased the last traces of juice from the plate.

"I'm testing bio-chemical solvents," Em said, turning back to pull a sample of the treated saltwater up into a dropper. The shifting gradient in the tank began to undifferentiate. "Altering the genes of microbes, making them hardier, the ones that already digest poly-base substances." She glanced back at Sana. "Plastics."

Sana blinked, lowering the plate. She licked juice from her lips, suddenly suspicious. "Why are you telling me?"

"It's a stopgap," said Em, ignoring her, "but one that might buy precious time."

She swung her legs around the bench, walking to stand over Sana. Her dark eyes studied her for a long moment, then, like a seabird darting down to capture prey, she reached out to unlock Sana's handcuff.

"Why?" Sana asked, narrowing her eyes as Em entered the code to release her cuff, mind flicking again to the possibility that the fish was poisoned—why else tell her everything? Why else let her go?

"You're right," said Em. "I don't like you."

It didn't make much sense, as far as reasons went, but it also didn't really matter. Poisoned or not, all that mattered now was escape. Anything immediate would've been too obvious, and impossible besides. No, what Sana needed was an opportunity, and, more than that, an excuse.

She started to grab the rest of her things off the table, but Em blocked her way.

"Move."

"The experiments will be over in a few days," said Em, not in answer.

Sana glanced around for the gun she knew must be hidden somewhere. "Don't be ridiculous," said Em, maybe also remembering what happened last time.

She let out a growl of frustration. "Why let me go if you're still just going to keep me locked up in here?"

"You're insufferable," she said, taking a step toward her.

Sana held her ground. "You're exasperating."

They parried words like daggers, up close, until they were nose to nose. Until Sana could taste the salty tang of spit flying off her lips.

"You're incorrigible."

"You're delusional."

"You're intolerable," said Em.

Then Em's lips were on hers, hands on her neck and back, grabbing, pressing, searching. She wasn't sure who moved first, who kissed who, or if it was some inescapable pull that drew them together. She just knew their bodies were pressed flush, and she could still taste the last traces of saltwater on Em's lips as they moved against hers. She just knew they were finally moving, Em pulling her back through that door at the end of the room, down into a bunk—too small for two, but that didn't stop them.

Hands on hips, fingers digging. Her entire consciousness scaled down to only lips and tongues and teeth, pulling, snagging, tugging.

"You're insuppressible."

Sana didn't care anymore whether Em liked her or how much longer the experiments would last, because with her lips against her neck, it really didn't seem to matter.

***

"Everything is connected," she said, tracing the line of Sana's hip with her hand. "Everything."

Sana arched up to meet her as Em's hand moved even lower.

"Us. The oceans. Even all that plastic."

Sana shifted up to bite down sharply on her lip. Silencing her. "Stop talking," she demanded, and for once, Em did what she said.

***

The bunk was empty, covers rumpled, when Sana woke. She

slipped on an oversized shirt from the pile on the floor and ventured out, wearing little else.

"Dammit." Em slapped the flat of her palm against the table, sending ripples across the surface of the vials in front of her, a shifting gradient of colors, dark purple to white.

Sana watched her, eyes calculating as Em slid the microscope away, resting her head in her hands. Not the comforting type, Sana tapped her finger lightly against the table instead. A patter-pat of solidarity.

"Every scenario I run ends the same: the microbes just can't keep up. They eat and multiply but there's just too much of it."

"But they do eat it. So you've solved it then," said Sana, half questioning. Em didn't seem to take it as a comfort.

"It's not good enough."

Sana watched her, silently, measuring the lines of exhaustion around her eyes. "Come back to bed."

"I have to get this right," Em said, rubbing at a spot above her left eyebrow until it was red.

The glass of water from before was still there next to Sana's jacket, lying in a discarded heap on the floor. Sana crouched down, tracing her finger around the rim, before handing it off to Em.

Sana watched her take a sip, throat bobbing as her hand trailed down Em's shoulder to finally grab her by the hand. "Leave it for tonight," she said, and Em didn't notice the bottle of pills she let fall as she dragged her back to bed.

***

A single Lion's Mane Jellyfish drifted by the port window, its gelatinous pink body undulating with the pull of currents. Thirty-foot tentacles trailed by as it passed.

Sana slipped her hands through the sleeves of her leather jacket, shrugging it up over her back in a single practiced move. Stitches tugged uncomfortably at her shoulder, but she was planning to pull them out anyway—one less thing to slow her down. The vial of alprazolam was a small pressure against the flesh of her waist, back in the hidden pocket where it belonged.

The samples on the desk glowed iridescent blue in the low light, casting a soft shine through the tank of water that suffused out across the room. It was too bad, really, that Em had figured out the solution already. She fingered one of the sample vials, lifting it from the stand and twisting it through her fingers, watching the shift of light play through the glass.

Looked useless enough to Sana, but what did she know? How to manipulate people; how to do what was needed to get what she wanted. Em had her specialties. She had hers.

And it shouldn't matter, not really. If Em was telling the truth—if all she wanted was to save what was left out here—the means achieved the ends either way, whoever got the credit and, more important, the money.

She ripped off a page from the old notebook. In a few hours, when the benzodiazepine wore out of her system and Em awoke, hair frizzed from bed, hurt and confused, she'd find the unpracticed scrawl of Sana's note left in the center of the desk, mess cleared so she'd be sure to see: *24 hours.*

No endearments or promises—Em had been right when she'd called her selfish, and Sana had been even more right: the world was a selfish place. They both did what they had to—but Sana did one better.

Twenty-four hours. That was a generous head start, plenty of time for running or hiding or salvaging the rest of the samples before word got out. Plenty of time to make her choice, whatever it was. Sana owed her that much, which was saying something.

The people she worked for were going to take some convincing, and Sana couldn't show up empty-handed—not if she wanted to show up again at all. She pocketed the sample vial, grabbed a rebreather from the shelf.

No promises and no commitments. Just reality, and Sana swimming straight back to it.

Minor Mortalities
EJ Sidle

EJ Sidle likes coffee, cacti, and comics. She has a day job that takes up too many hours, and her housemate has four paws and doesn't contribute to rent. Currently, she lives in Scotland, but she's actually an Australian, so unlike her colleagues she still gets excited when it snows.

Theo Everett is not a hitman. Sure, he kills people for money, but he brings them back afterwards. Sometimes even more than once. He's an information extractor and mortality expert, nothing nearly as mundane as a simple assassin.

His target has lycanthropy. Alec Whitemore, a wolf who scented out something he shouldn't have and carried it all the way to the cops. Admirable, maybe even brave, but definitely stupid. At least Alec was bright enough to book a ticket out of town when his testimony didn't lead to conviction. Currently, he's having a panic attack in the window seat of Theo's row.

Fear is a powerful motivator, and a pungent odour. Theo can taste it in the back of his throat, the terror and panic palpable even to more human senses. Alec is drowning in it, passport crumpled in his fist and forehead pressing hard against the seat in front of him. Theo stares at him for a long moment, then carefully slides down into the aisle seat.

"Hey little wolf," he says evenly. Alec starts, entire body flinching and a growl quivering in his throat. It's not so much threatening as it is pathetic, and Theo sighs loudly. "I'm going to hand you something. Take it from me but don't break it."

He holds out a water bottle, waiting in silence until Alec

reaches out and snatches it. Theo watches as elongated claws flex around the shape, applying pressure but not crushing. Alec's breathing hitches.

"Good," Theo says. "I'm Theo. I want you to put your feet flat on the ground and push." There's a long pause, punctuated only by Alec's breathing, then the werewolf shudders and obeys.

"Are... are you using... magic?" Alec puffs through gritted teeth.

"No," Theo tells him. "Instructions. I'm making you focus on them instead."

"How do you know I'm a wolf?" Alec pants quietly.

"Your claws are out."

Alec huffs, sitting up slightly. "I'm Alec," he says, and smiles.

Theo thinks he's having a stroke. The air leaves the plane, and suddenly he can't hear anyone else around him. There's no passengers jostling each other, no children yelling, no flight attendants. Instead, there's Alec's breathing, steadier now, and the soft tethers that attach his soul to his body, strings that keep him with among the living. Theo almost reaches out to touch them, but he pauses at the last second and locks his arms to his side instead.

"Oh," Alec whispers, and the sound brings Theo crashing back into his own skin. The werewolf is still staring at him, eyes wide. "*Oh.*"

"Are *you* using magic?" Theo asks weakly. Alec shakes his head, tongue darting out over his mouth. Theo stares at it before cursing softly. "That's... unfortunate."

"I don't believe this," Alec mutters, not looking at him anymore.

"You just look at someone and there's a *connection*? A feeling? That's idiotic."

"What?"

"*Soulmates!*" Alec hisses, shaking his head. "Wolves are supposed to get soulmates."

"Little wolf," Theo says carefully. "I'm flattered. But, you were panicking and I was kind. That's all. It's a connection of circumstance."

"Yeah?" Alec scoffs, fingers tight around the water bottle. "Then why're you looking at me like you want to run me down?"

Theo rubs a hand over his eyes. "We need to get off this plane."

"What? Why?" Alec demands. Theo ignores him, standing and reaching over to pull Alec up. The werewolf flinches. "Why would I go with you?"

"Because," Theo hisses. "You put your nose where it didn't belong. You're a marked man."

"Shit!" Alec yelps, coming to his feet. "You're a cop?"

"Sure," Theo says, grabbing Alec's forearm and pulling him into the aisle.

There are still people stowing luggage. No one stops them, no one looks at them, and Theo drags the werewolf into the skybridge. The tunnel is small, enclosed, and for a moment Theo can taste the lives he's taken before. It's ash in his mouth, bile in his throat, and he feels his feet slowing.

"Hey, c'mon!" Alec pants, toothy grin flashing and water bottle still in his hand. "We're nearly there."

Theo isn't the only mortality expert on his boss' payroll. There's nowhere safe for the living.

He grabs Alec's shoulder, swinging them around until the werewolf's back collides with the wall. Alec winces, staring at Theo with wide eyes.

"They won't stop until you die," Theo says quietly. Alec's heartbeat kicks up, and Theo closes his eyes. "Little wolf, I need you to drink the water."

"Why?" Alec asks, glancing down at the bottle in his hand.

"Because," Theo says, gently rubbing a thumb across the skin of Alec's throat. "It's laced with wolfsbane."

Alec inhales sharply, expression impossibly betrayed. "Let me go," he whispers.

"Alec," Theo says. "We have a lot to talk about, but it can't be here. I can get you out but you need to trust me. Drink it."

"It's going to hurt!" Alec hisses.

"Yes. Then you'll be dead, and I'll report to my boss."

"Fuck off!" Alec snaps, trying to break free.

Theo slams him back against the wall of the skybridge. "Alec! If it's not me, it's someone else! And they won't be so nice about it."

Alec swallows, eyes flickering down to the hand on his throat, then up to Theo's mouth. His breath hitches. Theo pretends not to notice.

"Alec. Let me kill you. Your body moves easier without you in it. I'll get you somewhere safe, then put you back."

"I don't even know you," Alec says quietly, shaking his head.

"Then *trust me* and you might get a chance to," Theo says.

"Fine!" Alec snaps, dragging a hand through his hair. "Fuck! I can't believe I'm going to kiss a mage."

Theo blinks. "You don't have to."

"But I'm going to," Alec repeats. "As soon as you bring me back. So... don't lose me, alright?"

"Never," Theo promises softly. "Now drink."

Ganymede's Lamps
Michèle Laframboise

Michèle Laframboise feeds coffee grains to her garden plants, runs long distances and writes full-time. Fascinated by sciences and nature since she could walk, she holds advanced degrees in geography and engineering, and draws from her scientific background to create worlds filled with humor, invention and wonder.

Michèle has published 18 novels and about 45 SF short-stories in French and English, earning various distinctions in Canada and Europe.

Jupiter hung in the sky like a big round lava lamp.

Two bands were dancing through my ceiling window, the northern band's brown swirl invading the southern one's creamy texture, reminding me of Mom's morning cappuccino.

"No."

Jupiter's golden light crowned my mother's dark hair as she stood in my room, frowning. A flick of her hand had cut off the *Jumping Joseph Band* success that the walls were blaring.

Stupid walls.

Mom hated the *JJ Band*. They should have shut off the sound before she hopped in my room. Now the walls stayed silent, muted to a neutral gray.

A tinny residual hum rang in my eardrums.

"But, *Mom!* It will be my birthday!" I insisted.

She threw her multi-fingered hands up, as for cleaning up the ambient air. This was the wall scrubber's job anyway, as the fresh lilac smell wafting through my room confirmed. *A cloying stench of dead flowers,* Mom had said the first time, a tribute to our diverging sensory inputs.

"No, Beth," Mom repeated, crossing her arms to imprison her decision.

I hated it when she called me Beth, like taking a bet.

My proper name was Bethesda, a three-syllable melody on the lips of Uncle Gram. And my dolls, lined up in their pastel satin gowns on the shelf above my sleeping net, called me Betty, which was less offensive.

She uncrossed one arm to draw a circle in the air, her eight digits splayed like a fan.

"Maybe a mechanical model," she said.

My own fingers dug into the threads of the carpet, which had morphed into a neutral white as soon as it sensed my mother's steps approaching the room. (The walls had mindlessly continued to play my *JJ Band* compilation.)

This lukewarm concession did not appease me. I had received (and broken) oodles of mecha toys from Aunt Cally. I looked past Mom's face to the ceiling window. A strong orange curve was inching its way, pushing off the other bands. I hoped it was the Red Spot. (The "Red" spot was more like a dull orange, egg-shaped smudge, but I didn't get to choose the name.)

***

According to Ganymede's calendar, I was 565 years old. Old enough to know what I wanted!

"Why can't I have a *real* cat?" I asked. "I saw one on the news."

The carpet shivered under me, broadcasting waves of apprehension about cat-droppings to the Domo unit. Mom felt it, too. A smile displaced her frown.

"Even the carpet agrees," she said. "Think of the transport, the food, the vaccines, the maintenance…"

My fine-tuned ear detected the drag in her throat, a tiny spark of regret hovering under the radar.

"But I'm lonely, and you work all sort of hours!"

Mom shrugged under the widening strip of orange.

"You have your dolls."

I pursed my lips, so tight you can't see them.

Dolls, even the more expensive coming from Earth, had limited conversation skills, barely past a *how-do-you-do, Betty?* And *it's a nice day outside!*

That last reply was proof of the total goof-headiness of ignorant toy designers. On Ganymede, weather in our extra thin atmosphere ranged from soft particle winds to mighty Jovian magnetic storms, with a mean temperature of one hundred Kelvin degrees and a mean way of killing you if you got outside without a vacuum suit.

***

As we sat for supper, me still fuming inside from her refusal, a shrill magnetic alarm rose from our Domo unit.

All light and heat from the walls flickered off. The dull Zen music they had been playing dwindled to silence. The carpet's strands flopped down (like a wind-swept prairie, Mom had said once).

Mom sighed. She had planned to watch a drama tonight. Living close to a giant spinning lava lamp meant Jupiter's powerful magnetic fields played havoc with electronic circuits.

All children knew the drill. I hurried to my room and slipped inside my insulated overalls sporting a Hammer Goddess figure (my favorite heroine), and put on my gloves. The room temperature was falling fast despite the layers of foam lining the ceiling.

Blue flashes lit my room. I grabbed my window's handles and pressed my face against the bioglass.

Giant blue auroras painted the sky around the fragmented outline of Exec Tower. The tower looked like a pointed nose jutting up from Gany City, its patchwork face pierced with a thousand eyes.

Two of those eyes belonged to our tiny apartment near the face's perimeter.

Aunt Cally told me that only the cream of the cream (one of her funny coffee expressions) lived on Exec Tower, with side windows looking over endless ice plains. Aunt Cally worked as an office helper for the execs and Dominus, Gany-City's artificial mind watching over all Domos.

But what help a mere ten-digit adult could give I had no idea.

***

My eleventh birthday in Old-Earth years coincided with a Spot day. (For all its hugeness, Jupiter rotated fast -- less than ten hours -- but its turbulent clouds liked to play. The Spot, a stable storm, moved counterclockwise in six standard days, so its period makes one of our weeks.)

The Spot crossing the disk of Jupiter overhead signaled a day of pause for the human workers.

The robots did not mind because they had none.

The tower executives did not mind either, because they had too much of it. They were "not-all-there", as Uncle Gram said, as they were linked to the vaster mind of Dominus.

Technically, I had no father, since Mom gave birth to me by medic-assist. But I had more than enough uncles and aunts to make up for this absence.

On my birthday, Mom's coworkers, ice-diggers and core-digger remote pilots, crowded our living room, spilling in the hallway. Their eight-digit hands maneuvered with ease the complex handles of ice- and core-digging machines. All functioned with good-ol' analog systems and wires and crude radio transmissions, a must with the constant magnetic lashings from the Big Lava Lamp.

My birthday banquet featured braised salmon, lots of biscuits and my favorite pudding.

As Mom was reaching for a serving spoon, the large bowl of vanilla pudding shivered. A low rumble rose, as the ground shook. Everyone fell silent as Ganymede's ice cover shifted.

Ice quakes produced tremendous energy jolts, captured by cables plunging into Ganymede's entrails. So, when the tremors died away, Uncle Gram, a cable-digger remote pilot, lifted his punch glass.

"To Mother Ice!" he toasted, before draining his glass.

"Movement equals energy," Aunt Cally recited, beaming with pride.

Everyone followed suit, except Mom who looked at her pudding bowl. A skilled ice-digger pilot, she worked for Gany City Water Management. Every seism meant that she would have to repair the kilometers-long water pipes siphoning the under-ice ocean.

***

Uncle Gram swirled his long glass of champagne, slowly so the weak gravity wouldn't upset the liquid. He was back from his annual vacations on Europa, and had brought lots of shiny snippets he distributed around. His face was lined like Old Mars, with reddish-brown ridges and canyons circling around his cerulean eyes.

Said cerulean eyes locked on me, as I was finishing a chocolate-chips cookie. (Real chocolate, which must have dug a hole in Mom's budget.) Crumbs falling on the carpet were carried by slow undulations to a disposal chute near the wall. The carpet was busy, as most of Mom's colleagues had departed for more adult pastimes. Aunt Cally who didn't have many friends, had stayed.

"So, Bethesda," Uncle Gram said. "Have you been good while I was away?"

Every cell of my body echoed my resounding, "Yes, Uncle!" He had used my full name; my heart could have melted Ganymede's ice.

He presented me with a red-wrapped parcel.

I had not enough of ten fingers to unwrap my present. The gauze and padding kept shifting, the ribbon reforming its bows until I found the correct speed and gestures to open it.

It was a golden half-globe, like a salad bowl turned over, topped with three faceted eyes sparkling like dark amethysts. I took the toy in my hands, feeling the serrated edge along the rim. The domed surface was hard as metal, but underneath, the soft underbelly showed ridges and folds.

"Mind the legs", Uncle Gram said. "That thing was just unfrozen yesterday."

The serrated edge was moving: hundreds of tiny crochets searching purchase on my fingers. Excited, I crossed to my room and put down my new gift on the carpet.

That's when Domo went berserk.

Red letters erupted on the creamy carpet, warnings flashing as fast as the thread photocells could follow Domo's impulse.

"Intruder alert. Alien life form detected. Sterilization recommended."

Every warning was repeated by the walls. (Walls *were* stupid, but needed.)

"Oh, you old fool!" Mom exclaimed. "You didn't tell me it was alive!"

Uncle Gram had the good grace of looking concerned as Mom flicked her fan of fingers to tone down Domo's voice. Another flick signaled that the warning had been taken "into consideration."

You couldn't ignore a domestic guardian's warning. The safety of an entire city could be in jeopardy. But "taking into consideration" was acceptable, as long as we were unharmed.

"Well, Lucy," Uncle Gram said, "those lava lamps are all the rage on Europa and even Titan. They were gifted by those alien visitors from Sirius-B."

"And the microbes? We could be all dead!"

Uncle raised his hands in a placating stance, each palm wide enough to support eight long fingers.

"Naaah," he said. "You worry too much. Nobody died from having them."

Mom wrinkled her nose, even if scrubbers would have neutered any foul odor in the room.

"And what do those... things eat?" she asked.

Another flourish of Gram's eight-digit hand.

"You see, they don't need food. Just a lil' heat, a pinch of energy, and they can light up for weeks!"

I was considering the half globe sitting on the carpet. The strands were still struggling to carry the new arrival to the disposal chute. Tiny clamps dug into the carpet.

"Light up?" Mom repeated.

Just on cue, the salad bowl's skin glowed. Everyone fell silent. It glowed first in the reds, then the orange until it settled for a yellow-white light, the eyes' ruby tint changing to a warm red. The carpet had ceased struggling, its threads arcing away from my present.

The half-globe set in motion.

It ponderously crossed the floor then crept up the nearest wall, stopping its ascension at eye level.

"Lights off," Gram said.

A wave from Mom confirmed the order.

Obediently, the walls and ceiling dimmed their light. The warm golden glow of the lamp competed with the light from Jupiter overhead.

I was bursting inside, like the day I aced all the tests to qualify for additional fingers. (I would have to wait until fully grown, though.)

I could see the lines on Mom's forehead smoothing out. She had that dreamy, faraway look, when she remembered good times from before she migrated here.

Uncle Gram was smiling, too, his eyes closed. You would say a snowstorm had smoothed over his face.

Aunt Cally stated the obvious, shaking her cloud of red curls.

"What a nice little lamp!"

"Yup!" Uncle Gram said. "It's supposed to respond to your moods," he said, looking at my mother.

"My mood would be to pound your stupid head against the wall to check which would be the hardest," Mom said.

But she was smiling as she said it.

***

My lava lamp had acclimated itself.

After the birthday, Mom and uncle Gram adjusted Domo to ignore our new guest's organic presence. No known pathogens had been detected on its golden shell. As for the inner flora, the organism was remarkably self-contained.

The lamp did not poop on the floor, to the huge relief of the carpet whose color returned to an earthy beige.

The lamp's output varied, following my moods or the music played by the walls.

How it could sense moods I didn't know. Uncle Gram talked about body heat and pheromones and limbic systems and this and that.

Aunt Cally talked about spiritual waves and Zen.

All was well on Gany City.

For a time.

***

The first disquieting sign was the disappearance of my lamp. One evening the salad bowl was glowing over my net, the next morning it was gone.

You couldn't hide in a small apartment like ours. Contrary to a ton of old stories, ventilating conducts were too narrow, even for a salad-bowl lava lamp with tiny legs.

I felt down, unhappy. The uniform lightning from the (stupid, inattentive) wall was not the same.

My dolls' boring conversations did not lift my spirits. To be honest, since the lamp shone up on my life, the dolls had receded in shadows. They were now lined on the higher ledge, assorted rainbow-like in their pastel gowns.

***

Uncle Gram told me pets ran away sometimes. Mom covered her face with sixteen slender fingers.

Two days later, to my relief, I found my lamp hugging the round window's edge, its mottled shell almost undistinguishable. I wondered why it had disappeared.

Later still, before Spot Day, my left foot struck a small bump on my green carpet. You would think someone had slipped a golf ball under it, but the carpet was organically tied to the floor. You couldn't slide a nail under it. And the floor itself was molded over the ice foundations of Gany City.

The carpet threads strained in vain to cover the mound.

***

The mound had grown from golf ball-sized to tennis ball-sized when Mom tripped on it.

After a long day of directing a digger under a stubborn layer of hexagonal ice to find the pesky ocean, her mood flared like a magnetic storm.

"What in the *quake* is that?"

She pushed herself back up with such anger that she drifted to the ceiling.

Domo could not help, as Mom's tinkering had rendered the domestic intelligence blind to the lamp.

But she knew where to ask.

Uncle Gram bought six minutes of Dominus' time to communicate with Europa. He couldn't trace the guy who sold him the lamp, but he consulted with his friends there. While we waited for his buddies to come back with some answers, the carpet mound had accrued its girth to a familiar salad-bowl shape...

The carpet around it had paled from a luscious green to a dull white.

***

Ten days after my birthday, the carpet strands holding the half-sphere broke, one by one, revealing a dark orange shade.

I was witnessing the birth of a new lamp when I heard Mom trip and fall.

"*Quaaake!*" she cursed.

I rushed into the living room. Mom was tenting her scalded fingers. The carpet was absorbing the brown coffee splash, its threads carrying the (intact but empty) cup away.

Between Mom's feet, sure enough, I recognized a small bump, like a hidden golf ball...

"Stay in my room," she said in a stern alto voice. "I will get ahold of your uncle."

Mom didn't dare use the com system, not after tampering with Domo. She had to go in person. She exited the apartment and jumped to the nearest handhold. Then Mom propelled herself away, faster than she could walk.

***

Uncle Gram put down his useless hammer. (He was no Hammer Goddess!) Mom considered the various pieces of tools that had bent, broken, or shattered upon impact. The two of them were sweating profusely, prodding the walls to scrub harder.

Stupid walls; the powerful lemon smell they released to counter the sweat was irritating my nose.

"By Jove!" Uncle Gram panted. "This critter has the sturdiest organic shield I ever saw!"

"Can we cut the wall?"

He pivoted to face me.

"Are you out of your mind, girl?"

His voice had taken an irritated tone I had never heard from him before.

Besides being stupid, our walls were connected to Domo, which was in turn connected to Dominus. Cutting an inner wall would raise alerts and questions. (As for even *touching* the thick perimeter walls protecting us against frozen death, it was a big no-no.)

The last thing Mom needed was to draw the attention of the Exec Tower to her domestic worries.

***

A full week-long orbit later, eight lamps were variously scattered in our apartment, their shells ignoring any attempts to break them, their out-of-reach insides and/or brains ignoring any coaxing, pleading, threat, whatever.

"Uncle, do you think it's an invasion?"

Wall-screen's stories had invaded my imagination. Uncle Gram snorted, spilling his coffee. His Europan buddies had not talked back to him.

The carpet needed more time to absorb the coffee stains, its surface toned down to a dull gray. The adjusted Domo was unaware of its plight.

As for the walls, the anchored lamps slowed them so much I had to wait a full dorky minute to hear my favorite *JJ Band* song.

Our prospects were grim, as Hammer Goddess would say.

***

Finally, Aunt Cally spilled the beans or, in her clumsy ten-digits case, the coffee as she tripped on, yes, another rounded protrusion.

"My boss told me yesterday how funny lamps like yours were multiplying everywhere on the other worlds."

Even if she hadn't the nimblest fingers in Gany City, she couldn't help noticing *twelve* hanging lamps dispensing their golden light around the living-room.

"Europa has declared a full quarantine," Aunt Cally said, shivering. (The stupid walls had quit lighting up and barely kept us warm.)

She swallowed in one loud gulp the nice swirls Mom had carefully laid on her second cappuccino.

"This explains why I can't reach my buddies!" Uncle Gram said, downing his cup.

Aunt Cally lifted her curly head to the ceiling.

"I, I think we should call up my boss," she said.

***

Aunt Cally's boss was a formidable woman, iron-haired and iron-willed, who never flinched at the words "battle ax" thrown at her by disgruntled employees.

All those formidable qualities were concealed under a chocolate pudding body that would get crushed into a chocolate puddle if she dared walk on Earth's surface.

Big Martha waddled from room to living-room, hemming and hawing at the indifferent lamps, while Mom sat, her head hanging down like a switched-off light. Uncle Gram didn't fare better, but he kept a lid on his emotions, his cerulean eyes gazing up at the dark face of Jupiter.

He and Mom looked like two children at fault. Under any other circumstances, the picture would have made me laugh.

Big Martha plumped herself down the sofa. When the two stopped quivering, she spoke.

"Gany City's energy budget has declined since three weeks," she said.

Her voice was a surprisingly cool soprano.

"I guess that would coincide with Mr. Gram Edison's return from his vacation."

Uncle Gram nodded, his lips pressed in a thin crack.

I had been more worried about him or Mom losing their job than any danger the lamps presented. Now, with more adults crowding the room (Big Martha had come with assistants), moving around the lamps, marking them with blotches of black paint, measuring energy fluxes and magnetic fields and shell's photo spectroscopy), I had to reconsider.

***

Two cups of *very* well-topped cappuccinos later, Big Martha ticked off the conclusions on the stubby (but well-manicured) fingers of her left hand.

"First, I salute Ms. Calliente Almond for warning the city's authorities of the threat."

Aunt Cally, unused to be on the receiving end of compliments, blushed under her cloud of curls.

"Second, those living lava lamps, while bereft of hostile intention, drain too much energy from the city grid."

Uncle Gram's head hung lower. So much for his, "They don't need a lot" selling point!

"Third, we suspect those lamps are part of a planned disruption of our viable colonies. Recent communications have revealed that the lamps proliferation had ravaged our sapient visitors' own planets before they managed to put a stop to it."

Uncle Gram sat up.

"Oh yeah?"

"How did they stop the lamps?" I asked.

A lopsided smile creased Big Martha's face.

"Nuclear eradication of all contaminated areas," she said, ticking off a finger. "Which was, young lady, my fourth point."

Mom gaped, her cappuccino shivering. Aunt Cally let out a small gasp. Even if they were mean to us, I felt sorry for the sapient visitors. I hoped they got their people out *before* nuking the cities.

"Five," Big Martha said, "the lamps sold to unsuspecting bozos (a nod to Uncle Gram who was now studying his shoes) originated from a world where they stood at the lowest rung of the food ladder. So those life forms developed a fierce passive defense, their shell incredibly resistant, while sucking sun rays, energy from landslides, quakes, natural electricity..."

"Like a thunderstorm?" I asked. "I saw those on the Knowledge Canal."

"Yes."

Aunt Cally's boss looked at an almost ripe lump on the carpet, while the technicians were muttering between themselves.

"My next point," she said, ticking off her sixth finger, "is that the visitors, while transiting between worlds, kept the lamps on the outside hull of their vessels."

"So, they could survive at absolute zero?" I blurted.

Uncle Gram piped in.

"In space, the mean temperature is three Kelvin degrees, Bethesda."

"Yeah, I know," I said. "The fossil radiation and yadda yadda..."

"Ahem!" Aunt Cally interrupted.

Big Martha ticked off the seventh finger of her left hand.

"According to Dominus, the City's energy budget is tottering along, thanks to the latest magnetic storm."

"But," she said, ticking her last finger. "We must find a way to stop the multiplication before those critters upset the energy balance of our City in their favor."

***

Two new lamps had emerged from the ailing carpet when Mom was called to the Exec tower offices.

I went with her. Aunt Cally met us at the lifts, with a reluctant Uncle Gram.

The summit of Exec tower rose a gasping forty floors over the city roofs. The transparent wall of the lift showed my pale reflection, next to Aunt Cally's cloud of hair, dark strands swirling like Jupiter's clouds. Mom was turned away, her arms crossed so tight her elbows were covered by white knuckles.

I pressed my nose against the insulated glass (leaving a moist oval after), taking in the long rusty cracks fleeing toward a gray horizon, crossing and re-crossing themselves like my baby drawings.

I searched down for my little round window among thousands of similar portholes, but without mapping goggles, it was no use.

***

Big Martha's office was on the 39th floor. Over her floor, Aunt Cally had proudly explained in the lift, sat the com array of Gany City.

And Dominus.

You'd think that such sensible apparatus would be kept hidden deep below ground. Except that Ganymede was made of layers of ice.

Moving ice.

So, the heart and lungs of Gany City hovered at a lofty height, enclosed in a light metallic meshing, looking like a floating gray bubble atop a needle.

"We have sealed your apartment," Big Martha was saying.

"But, we, my things," Mom said, stammering.

Big Martha raised her wide palm: a screen unfolded from the desk. It was funny to recognize my X-rayed body, Uncle Gram's long frame, Mom's arm-crossed stance, and Aunt Cally stooped posture.

Taken while we were in the lift.

"You were all screened and found clean."

"You screened us?" Mom said, having a great appreciation of her privacy.

"Necessary. Because those critters have spread outside your unit."

I cringed at my birthday present called a critter. Mom uncrossed her arms.

"What? Impossible!"

"How many times did you go in and out while the lamps were growing inside your unit?"

A loud clap of both eight-digit hands raised another screen. I recognized the portion of corridor outside our unit. Two lumps were budding on the bare polymeric floor.

Aunt Cally gasped aloud.

"They're spreading," she obvious-stated.

Big Martha looked at her helper, sighed, and then showed

143

another view of the corridor. A circle of spikes protruded from the wall abutting my room.

My birthday lamp was rooting in.

"Those little teeth at the base can cut through metal," Big Martha said. "It will take time, but eventually they will succeed and take over Gany City."

"We're fortunate the critters don't feed from our own organic electricity," Uncle Gram mused.

"If only we could rip those lamps from the walls," Mom said.

Martha spread her brown fan-like fingers.

"We tried," she said. "Nada. Once they set their grip, it's like those alligator's teeth: no way to make them let go."

Except by nuking them.

"So, are you, are we... (*Mom paused to swallow*) considering an evacuation of Gany City?"

A big lump clogged my throat. Evacuating Gany City meant leaving Ganymede, the only home I had ever known.

Uncle Gram put his fanned hand on Mom's shoulder.

"We will find something, Lucy, I swear," he said.

"Is there any other way besides nuking them?" Mom asked, looking sideways at me.

Martha shrugged.

"*If* we could extract the lamps from the walls, and *if* we could put them in a place devoid of any form of available energy, they would die of deprivation," she stated.

While the adults talked, I gazed at the landscape through the windows.

From this height, I could see more of the ice faults, and far away ridges, judging their relative ages by the width and color. I followed the cracks with my eyes until the moon curvature hid them, picturing their path on the other side, like a dried-out apple skin.

My eye was drawn to a big rope cutting the view. Vertical iron cables along the Tower's hull harvested Ganymede's powerful magnetic field, as Aunt Cally had explained.

"Movement equals energy," she had recited at my birthday party.

And more of that energy was carried by ice cracks.

I peered at the fleeing ridges while the conversations —the one we had had before, the one occurring here— mingled in my brain.

I didn't want to kill my birthday present. The salad-bowl lamps were not conscious of their wrongdoings. They lived; they prospered.

Their prospering would force us to leave.

And so, aimlessly looking at a crack so old it disappeared under the others, an answer rose inside me like magma spurting up a volcanic chimney.

***

Uncle Gram disentangled his many fingers from the hexadecimal handles. The pads at the tips of his fingers were deformed by years of use to control remote diggers.

"It's ready," he said.

My vac-suit hung on the communal peg, a light blue all-in-one affair with an air reserve.

"Are you sure you want to do it, Bethesda?"

I ran my fingers around the hermetic band at the base of my helmet to check for anomalies. I hadn't been outside often, but all children of Ganymede learned to check and enter a vac-suit before the age of five, and the toddlers were trained to slither inside an emergency air bubble at the sound of an air break alarm.

"Yes, Uncle," I said.

I lowered the helmet over my head, adding tones of orange over all the ambient colors, changing the paleness of Aunt Cally's face, as she gripped the controls of her screen, where a single red point shone.

"After all," I said, "they're my birthday present."

Mom inched closer.

"Let's go, Beth," she said, her numerous fingers fastening her gray helmet. "And pray the universe your fool uncle—"

I lost the rest when her helmet sealed shut.

Uncle Gram closed the airlock door behind us, his long face scrunched in a contrite expression.

***

I would have loved to hear the dry crackling of the ice under my boots. But the surface was so hard that my steps would not produce any sound, especially in the thin Ganymede atmosphere.

Mom and I stood on the ice, looking up at the curving wall of Gany-City.

Projectors, windows, and moving cams wove a light pattern pointing up, like those 3D grid diagrams. The exec tower pointed like an arrow to pierce Jupiter's heart. This time, the gas giant was a dark circle blotting out the stars directly overhead.

We waited, in silence. I was afraid the plan would not work.

Mom tapped my right shoulder plate.

Here it was, a shiny spider clop-clopping towards us, ice crystals flowing away from the sturdy meshed net it was dragging. The digger stopped four meters from the wall.

Inside the meshing, a sausage-like battery bigger than my own body radiated a powerful heat.

Mom and I waited, again. The second part of The Plan had been rehearsed and refined countless times since I interrupted the adults' conversation in Big Martha's office.

**

Having been apprised of the situation, Dominus politely asked to be switched off. The last transmitted com I received was of Big Martha answering *yes*.

My screen went black.

The whole grid went off-line. All over Gany City, myriads of windows blinked out.

Diggers stopped digging.

Domos stopped watching.

Carpets stopped managing wastes.

Walls stopped being stupid.

(They also stopped playing music, ventilating, scrubbing, filtering and heating.)

In that state, the one-hundred Kelvin degrees drafts would batter the structures. Heat and oxygen would seep out by the tiniest unrepaired defects. I picture all citizens wrapped in their insulated suits, relocated in the big mall under the Exec Tower.

Gany City would freeze in less than a standard day.

Now, the sole energy source on all Ganymede was oozing from the heat generator in the digger's net, plus a very faint leak from our vac-suits.

***

Gany City technicians had left our apartment's door open, while closing a whole section. The quickest way out for the energy-deprived lamps would be our ceiling windows.

Mom banded her knees.

She leapt off the ice, her hammer's long handle in hand, looking for a moment like Hammer Goddess, less the blond hair. She landed on the first row of roofs.

I followed her up. My muscles were not as strong, but I managed to grab the edge, and roll over the roof.

From my position, the city was one continuous plain rising to meet the Tower.

Mom could locate our apartment from memory, but I had no problem finding our room and living room windows. Their faint yellow glow lit Ganymede's thin atmosphere.

We leaped toward the light. Mom was there before me.

I bent over the rim of the window.

I recognized my room's colorless carpet, the shelf with my row of talking dolls in their muslin dresses. New lamps were hanging from the wall, dispensing their light among themselves.

For comfort?

Mom braced one boot on the window's edge. As she was poised to strike, I put a hand on her arm. I looked at her, pointing at the hammer.

The tool would weight over 100 kilograms on Earth; the head was tapered to ensure a maximal impact. (*Of course*, Mom's coworkers and Uncle Gram had offered to do the chore, but Mom felt that blindly accepting the gift had been her own fault, and Uncle's nimble fingers were the best to remote-program a digger.)

Whatever. I had to go, too.

Those lamps were, ultimately, my responsibility.

The hammer handle tapped like a butterfly on my glove. Mom took one step back, a rare smile lifting her cheeks. *Go first*, she signed.

I grabbed the handle.

Channeling my inner Hammer Goddess, I lifted the heavy

weapon high over my head. I spared one thought for the beautiful half-spheres who wanted only to make more children, and one half-thought for my dolls who wanted only to talk.

Then I brought down the hammer with all my might.

I heard only my ragged breath. I did not break anything, but a crack had appeared on the glass. (We built to last on Ganymede; the anti-meteor shutters would have closed over the window if the Domo was online.)

My arms stinging from the shock, I made another attempt. My blow barely grazed the surface.

Mom signaled with a gloved fan to back off. She closed all her fingers on the handle and hefted the thing higher that I did. In the faint light of the stars, I saw tears streaming on her cheeks.

Then she struck, her speed and strength multiplied by her anger.

In total silence, the glass shattered, a crystal fountain rising high as pressurized air escaped from what had been our home.

Many objects followed. Coffee cups forgotten on the counter; underwear forgotten on Mom's bed…

My dolls took flight in their windblown gowns, tiny arms pointing away, disappearing amidst the stars.

***

Part three of The Plan would now go into motion. Uncle Gram's digger vibrated, augmenting the call of the heated cell. The hardest part of the plan for Mom and me was to shut down our own life-systems. Our oxygen feed came from a mechanical pressure valve.

The cold began to seep in my fingers and toes.

I shivered. The possibility of losing fingers to the frost loomed over my head like Jupiter's dark disk. We knew there would be a delay; Uncle Gram and Aunt Callie had made computation after computation, based on the techs' measurements...

Mom tapped my shoulder.

One tiny claw at the time, a glowing lamp slowly uprooted itself from the wall.

Mom pushed me back as one, then two lamps crept up the wall, then negotiated the broken window. The odd angle let me see the underside. A reddish knot of roots or tentacles had pierced the wall as easily as moist earth.

We kept a good fifty meters away from the procession of lamps towards Gany City's outer wall.

Mom moved. She jacked something between us, a loud *click*.

"Can you hear me?"

Her voice filled my ears. Only then was I aware of how the silence had made me feel lonely.

"Mom? But the power will..."

"It's only an acoustic hose between our two suits. No power."

The first golden half-ball reached the edge. I made out a trace of black paint on its shell, a zero. It was the primary lamp, my birthday gift!

It went over the edge and tipped down, its light wavering, failing.

I shut my eyes by reflex, not wanting to witness its demise. But then, I remembered how uncle Gram's effort had shown their uncanny resistance. I opened wide, in time to see it bouncing back over the ice, the low gravity lending an eerie grace to its moves.

We were close enough from the edge to see it tottering on the cold ice, towards the beacon of heat calling from the frozen vastness.

Another bright lamp slid off the edge and tumbled down.

That one landed like a terrain turtle, on its shell. It couldn't get upright alone. As more lamps came down, three of them scuttered over their comrade and lifted one side, to let it tumble right.

I checked our window, to make sure no one was left behind.

"They all went out," Mom said. "I counted the 57 of them."

Soon, a procession of lamps was trudging on the ice toward the digger, some trailing the very small ones cut free from the carpet.

The hungry lamps did not reach the spiderlike machine.

Its mechanical legs began backing away from the City, trailing the heat-emitter battery behind it. I felt sorry for the lamps, like those children led away from their homes by a musician in a story written so long ago.

The line of golden lights edged toward the horizon, their glow waning.

"Mom, the lamps... Are you sure...? They..."

Words failed me. A warm drop coursed down my cheek.

"You're not killing them, honey", Mom said.

I began sobbing, a no-no in a vac suit. I couldn't reach for my face. I felt the pressure of Mom's embrace.

"Your lamps won't die," she said. "And I'm so proud of you, my dear, sweet *Bethesda*."

I blinked, hard.

The digger would lead the lamps into a deep hollow, on the other side of the moon. The gallant machine would stay with them until its own battery emptied out.

The temperatures there would never rise over one hundred K: all lamps would enter a low-energy cycle. They would feed from magnetic and seismic waves, enough for the present kid-lamps to grow, but not enough to reproduce.

They would stay alive, forever.

Or until we found a way to scoop them up and send them back to their own home.

***

I blew the twelve wax candles in our new apartment at the base of the tower. The wax candles were a luxury Mom could now afford. Big Martha and Aunt Cally smiled, each holding a fuming cup of cappuccino with beautiful swirls, served by Uncle Gram.

Two large windows graced our new unit, ceiling and sideway.

Every day, I gazed at the crisscrossing lines fleeing toward the horizon. Every week, while studying, I observed the Sun rising and setting. I worked hard to become an exobiologist.

A run-of-the-mill, ten-digits one.

Sometimes, as I worked on practice tests, I would glimpse a golden glow over the dark horizon line. Uncle Gram said it was the ice refracting up our thin atmosphere.

He didn't believe it, and neither did I.

Mom came back, holding a wrapped box in all her fingers. She lowered the gift on my knees.

I lifted the box. It was heavier than I expected. I undid the yellow wrappings. Not too fast, because of what came out of this action last time.

Relieved, I fingered a square metallic box, tubes and dials indicative of a self-contained environmental unit. Two shiny copper latches held the lid.

Big Martha waved one multi-fingered hand.

"Come on, open it, girl!"

I undid the latches. *Click. Clack.* The lid sprang open. A visible puff of moisture and a stuffy-room smell wafted out.

Then, from inside the box, a sound rose, truly alien on Ganymede.

"*Miaaaaw?*"

The White Place
Dana Berube

Boston-based writer, artist, large glasses enthusiast.

Ti awoke in the John's bed, blinking in the soft morning light, and thought, *Thank God.* The blizzard was still roaring outside, thrashing the house with pellets of ice, but the man's bed was warm, his blankets soft. Clean; no bugs. Compared to the haylofts and flophouses where he usually slept, it was heavenly.

The old man snored beside him, his back a slab of mole-pocked pink. He was old enough to be Ti's grandfather, but it hadn't been so bad. He'd been gentle and nervous, and far more courteous than the men usually were when they took him home from whatever godforsaken tavern or alley they'd found him in. And, Ti hadn't had to spend the night outside in that storm. That was all that really mattered.

It had been a near thing too. Two days ago, he'd trudged out of the hills with just his bag and the clothes on his back, hoping desperately that this place, and these people, would be different from all the others. They weren't. There was no welcome and no work here for a ragged transient, or at least none that someone like him could do safely. His one offer, shoveling horseshit out of a barn, was too risky—horses could sense his strangeness, and that would bring trouble from humans. By yesterday evening, with snow spitting and his empty stomach gnawing, he'd resigned himself to what he needed to do. Back to a tavern, back to a seat at the counter where everyone could see how young and handsome and available he was. He spent his last two coins on a pint, undid the top two buttons of his shirt, and lay in wait.

It had taken the old man in the corner a while to work up his courage. This was the kingdom's heartland, where the Church's word was law, the Ordermen were merciless, and the neighbors were nosy. A man with certain tastes had to be discreet, careful.

Not unlike a wizard.

Ti had been faint with hunger by the time his glances and smiles finally coaxed the man over, but his patience paid off. The old man's paunch, the book under his arm, and his neat shirt and waistcoat spoke of a desk job, modest wealth, and a well-kept home. Jackpot. He bought Ti dinner, so Ti went home with him and fucked him.

The man had said his name was Berron, as if it mattered.

Last night's pints drove him from the warmth of the bed. Careful not to wake the man, he slid out from beneath the blankets, wrapped himself in a robe, and padded from the bedroom. The grandfather clock in the hallway said it was just past eight. Tacked to the lintel of the doorway into the kitchen was something he hadn't seen when they'd stumbled in the previous night: a saint's medallion with a twist of ribbon.

He froze, one bare foot in the hallway, the other hovering over the cold wood floor of the kitchen. It was a charm to repel wizards and protect the property from their magic. A common folk superstition, and in reality completely useless, except for reminding wizards that they were unwelcome. In case they ever forgot. There had been one nailed over Ti's head at the tavern last night too.

Finding one in a home like this wasn't unusual, but it was still a sharp prick into a wound that never healed. For a moment he considered incinerating the hateful thing with a twitch of his powers. No. The old man had no idea what he was, and he couldn't risk him finding out. They cut wizards to pieces in towns like this. Ti took a breath, passed under it, and went into the kitchen.

Outside, the wind was howling and tearing at the roof like a mad beast, but within, the house was silent but for the ticking clock. The man's home was tidy and well-furnished, with a number of empty rooms that suggested there might have been a wife and children once. He lived alone now, except for a tabby cat, but still kept his lamps polished and a linen cloth on his table. He wasn't rich, not the way Ti's family had been—back when he'd had a family. But, there was a cast-iron hand pump in the kitchen and a copper tub in the bathroom, and that was a luxury the likes of which Ti had not seen in a very long time.

It was an opportunity he couldn't pass up. As quietly as he could, he pumped water into a pitcher, carried it into the bathroom, and filled the tub. The tub was cold and the water colder, but he didn't know how much longer the man would sleep and didn't want to waste time heating water in the hearth. Still, to be cautious, he lit the hearth anyway and made absolutely certain the bathroom door was locked. Then he dunked his hand into the water, focused his thoughts and will, and converted a fistful of his magic into thermal energy.

Within a few minutes, the bathwater was steaming. Ti carefully stepped in, folded his long legs, and sat down. God, it was glorious. When had he last had a bath that wasn't in a bucket or a stream? There was even soap on a table beside the tub, along with a razor and a washcloth. He scrubbed every bit of himself, even between his toes, cleansing himself of the road and the old man's touch.

Clean. Warm. Safe, for now. Sighing, he closed his eyes. He forced his mind to be as still and empty as the house, to let every thought drain away until there was nothing left inside him but a blank, white place. It was something he'd learned to keep the past in the past and the future in the future. To escape from the present, too, when necessary. To feel nothing, be nothing.

As always, the noise and sharp edges of the world inevitably intruded on the white place. From the kitchen came the sound of someone knocking about, followed by the smell of toast and frying eggs. Ti got out of the tub, chilled the water to a non-suspicious temperature with another swirl of his fingers, and dried off. He found Berron setting two places at the kitchen table.

With his hair wet and his jaw freshly shaved, there was no hiding that he'd made use of the tub. "Sorry," he said.

The old man waved it off. "You're more than welcome! Here, I made breakfast."

They sat at the table with the white tablecloth, a little porcelain statue of St. Wynn the Benevolent between them, and ate their breakfast. The man was shy again, fumbling to make conversation. Ti listened politely, but said little. Somehow, this part was always more awkward than the fucking. The man's earnestness was endearing, though. Ti liked him.

The man took his clean plate and peered out the window. "I say, there has to be at least a foot already."

Ti helped clear the table, secreting the heel of the bread loaf into the robe pocket to take with him, then went into the bedroom to dress. The man watched from the doorway for a few moments before disappearing back into the kitchen. Ti wondered if he dared ask for some food to take with him. He didn't want to do that—it felt too much like asking for payment—but it was either that or steal a candlestick to pawn, and he hated doing that to the nice ones.

But when the man returned, he was carrying a small burlap bag of bread and cheese. "For the road," he said, and pressed it into Ti's hands, like a gift.

"Thank you," he said, with gratitude.

The man frowned through the curtains at the snow falling outside.

"Do you have somewhere to go?" he said.

Ti said nothing. In truth, he had no plan other than try to earn some coin shoveling snow—maybe move on to the next town, try to find another warm place to bed down for the night. He was packing up to leave primarily out of habit. The men always kicked him out first thing in the morning.

The old man trailed him through the house, wringing his hands, while Ti gathered his coat and bag.

"Thanks for breakfast," Ti said, and opened the front door.

The squall of wind was like a punch. The house shook, and Ti stepped back, snow stinging his eyes.

Berron put his arm across the doorway.

"Lad, I can't send you out in that," he said. "You'll freeze to death out there. If you were my son—"

His eyes widened as if he'd been stabbed. Ti was probably younger than his son. Ti didn't begrudge any of these men their needs, but he resented this moment—after their lust congealed to shame—when they turned paternal to stave off their guilt. Ti already had a father, and if he wasn't concerned about his son's well-being—and he wasn't—then who did these men think they were?

"I'll be fine."

"Please," the man said. "You're welcome to stay until the snow stops. It's just me and the cat here."

Ti looked out into the storm. The world was violent, swirling whiteness in every direction, so thick he could not see the other end of the street. Heading out into that on foot would be madness.

He heaved the door closed. "All right. Do you have a shovel? I'll clear the walk before it gets any higher. Earn my keep."

The old man chuckled, clearly relieved. "Lad, you've already more than earned your keep—"

"I'm not a whore," Ti snapped.

The man dropped his eyes to the floor. "Beg your pardon. I didn't mean to cause offense."

He went to a closet and dug out a shovel.

"Kind of you to offer," he said. "It's rough on my back these days. I'll make tea for when you're done."

Ti set down his bag, took the shovel, and went outside.

The whiteness engulfed him as he worked. The whole town was eerily silent, the streets empty. He threw himself into the practiced motions—scoop, lift, up and over—and tried to imagine the white silence filling him and obliterating everything. No thoughts, no memories, no fathers, only the cold, the crunch of the snow under his boots, the strain in his arms.

He wondered if it really made a difference if he asked for payment or not. He marveled that he still cared.

Soon he was sweating from the effort, the treasured cleanliness ruined. The irony struck him, as always: this would be so much quicker and easier with magic. If he didn't have to hide the peculiar energy interwoven through his veins, he could melt the snow and ice with heat and have the walkway cleared in under a minute. He could clear every street in town, for a fee, and make a decent living. If only he was allowed to use his magic. If it was not seen as dirty, unnatural, a deadly insult to God's Divine Order and the king's monopoly on force. Of course, the Church and the king thought the current way he earned his living was dirty and unnatural too, but there was a world of difference between being reviled and pitied and being reviled and feared.

Berron had black tea steeping on the stove when Ti came inside. He helped him out of his snow-fringed coat and hat and placed a warm mug in his hands. The old man chattered absently while Ti sipped. The cat sat on the table and accepted a scratch around the ears. Cats could always sense a wizard, but they didn't snitch.

The storm raged unabated for the rest of the day. The old man kept the fire in the study roaring, and they passed the time reading and playing chess. The man slipped in and out of fits of shyness, sometimes babbling to fill the silence, other times contentedly watching the fire. Ti, who could be very shy himself, didn't mind at all and spoke just enough to be companionable.

The few careful words he did say fascinated the old man. Berron was delighted to discover that Ti appreciated his small yet respectable library, but puzzled that his tavern boy was well-read in Ying philosophy and 13th century poetry. He remarked with wonder that Ti held his fork and knife like a well-bred gentleman. Whatever he inferred from this made him sigh and watch Ti with sad, soft eyes.

"Do you have a mother and father somewhere?" he asked, while they ate a dinner of stew and red wine.

"Somewhere."

Berron chose not to pry. "I don't even know your name."

"Tom."

The old man didn't seem surprised by the lie.

After dinner, they drank more wine and played another game of chess. Berron brought out an old bottle of Tannerly red, saved for a special occasion. When he was drunk and numb enough, Ti kissed the old man on the mouth and led him into the bedroom.

***

The storm continued for two more days.

"One for the history books!" Berron said, marveling through the curtains at the snow, which by the third afternoon was now as high as the windows and still falling. "Thank God you stayed. I would have been snowed in until spring otherwise. Would have had to toss the cat out with a message tied to his collar—*Help, send more wine!*"

"Ho!" he said with delight, catching Ti smiling. "That got a grin out of you, did it?"

Ti was grateful he'd stayed too. He wasn't sure what he would have done, caught out on the road in a storm like this. Gotten himself arrested by the Ordermen just to get a roof over his head? Berron's house was cozy and comfortable, and the old man had gone out of his way to make him feel welcome. They were quickly falling into a routine, like a real couple, with Berron cooking the meals and Ti shoveling and tending the fire.

He finished lacing his boots and stood. "I'd better get out there again."

Berron kissed him sweetly and squeezed his bicep. "Thank the saints for those strong arms of yours."

Outside, the neighborhood's row houses and little shops were no more than vague shapes under a thick white blanket, but the street was no longer silent. Voices and the crunch of shovels filtered through the curtains of tumbling flakes. Neighbors, waging their own war against the snow. A loud shriek nearby made Ti's heart stop, and for a split-second his entire being was nothing but a lightning bolt of *run fight hide*—but it was only a child playing in a drift.

He started in surprise a second time as what he initially took to be a bear plowed through the snow towards him.

"Afternoon," the bear said, with a nod. Upon closer inspection, he was a massive man with a wild black tangle of a beard. "Where's Berron?"

"Marius, hello!" said Berron's wide eyes from the crack of the doorway.

Marius waved a mittened paw. "Came to check on you, old man! Brought you some milk and bread. Are you going to invite me in or not?"

Berron stumbled over himself to open the door wider and beckon him inside. "O-oh, yes, of course, come in!" After a moment's hesitation he added, "You might as well come in, too, Tom."

Ti and Marius shook off their coats and boots on the threshold and followed him into the house. Berron sat them both down at the table and gathered cups and saucers for tea. Marius eyed Ti.

"I see you met my nephew," Berron said quickly. In his nervousness he nearly knocked Marius's cup off the table. "My sister's boy, from out east. Came for a visit. Not so lucky for him, getting caught in this weather, but quite fortunate for me!"

Marius shook Ti's hand, frowning a little.

The two men were neighbors and had known each other for thirty years, but the kitchen felt tight and uncomfortable. The clock ticked too loudly. Berron babbled about the storm and his back and the cat and avoided looking at his "nephew." Marius kept glancing at Ti, the furrow in his brow growing deeper and deeper as he worked through what he was seeing. Feeling the tension, Ti sipped his tea and kept his face carefully blank. He surreptitiously laced up his boots in case he needed to make a run for it.

Ultimately, Marius chose not to say anything. With his tea barely touched, he stood and said he ought to head home. Before he left, he shook Ti's hand again, squeezed his fingers cruelly, and gave him a look of disgust—as if it was his fault for leading the old man astray.

Well, fuck you too, Ti thought, wondering why *he* was always the disgusting one.

"Good man, that one," Berron said, closing the door after him and locking it. "Kind of him to check in on me. They worry about me, now that Mel's gone..." His words caught in his throat.

He went to the hearth to heat up more water. Ti waited silently for him to gather his thoughts about what they both knew had just happened.

"It's not an easy life," he said, his voice tight. "I made my decision. We were happy, me and Mel. We had a son. He's grown now, living all the way down in Haizhou. Mel passed three years ago. We had a good life together. I made my choice. I kept some things hidden. It would have been hard otherwise." He sighed and looked at Ti with sad brown eyes. "Well, I don't need to tell you that."

He thought he knew Ti's story—that his God-fearing family, upon discovering his proclivities, had cast him out to wander the kingdom penniless and alone. Ti could see the old man seeing his younger self in him and thinking, *that could have been me.* That wasn't Ti's story, or at least not the whole story, but the old man was trying. It was something.

Berron's eyes fell to his shoes. "I haven't—I've never done this sort of thing before."

"You don't have to explain yourself to me," Ti said, but internally he steeled himself for what was sure to come next. *I'm afraid I have to ask you to go, I've got my good name to think of...*

Instead, to his surprise, Berron came closer and swept a loose lock of Ti's hair behind his ear. The gesture was so tender and unexpected, Ti's white-knuckled stillness shattered. When Berron put his arms around him, Ti melted against his chest. He let himself be held as tight as a child and gripped the old man as if he were a life raft. The warm space between the soft arms and the woolen waistcoat smelled like soap and safety.

***

Late that night, they lay awake together under the covers. The snow had finally stopped, but the wind had grown even more bitterly cold. Ti, curled against Berron with his nose in the man's fuzzy grey chest hairs, was warm and sleepy. Berron stroked his hair, letting the long dark locks slide through his fingers. The cat dozed against the small of Ti's back.

"You could stay," Berron said softly in the dark. "For as long as you like. I could find you work in town."

Ti's heart beat fast, barely daring to believe what he was being offered. It would mean a place to stay, not for just one night or two, but indefinitely. His future, currently defined by his next meal, would again open up into days, weeks, months. He could make money and save it.

He could stay in the same town for more than a week. There would be someone who would notice if he did not come home. There would be a place to come home to. With time, safety, the space to think and to breathe, he could be a man again, rather than just a silent, agreeable body.

His silence made Berron nervous. "What are you thinking, my dear? I know it's a bit sudden, and I know I'm too old for you, but I'm alone here and I—well, I enjoy your company very much, Tom. I think we both have something to offer one another."

Ti raised himself on his elbow and kissed him.

"Ti," he said. "My name is Ti."

***

The next morning, the sky was a sheet of blue crystal, the air dry and bone-shatteringly cold. Only the thought of a hot bath roused Ti from the cozy cocoon of the bed, and only the promise to let Berron watch had stirred the old man.

But, when Berron tried to pump water for some tea first—they were not savages, after all—nothing came out.

"Oh no," he said. "Seems the pipe is frozen. Pray it hasn't burst, or we'll be melting snow until spring."

Ti frowned. He wanted that bath.

"I'll take a look," he said.

"Goodness, Ti, is there no end to your talents?" Berron said, giving his arm a squeeze.

Ti grinned. "You've never seen me try to dance."

He dressed and put on his coat and boots. Berron gave him a key, a wrench, and a shovel and directed him around the back of the house, where the pipes were accessible through a bulkhead.

Where he hadn't shoveled, the snow was more than waist-high. He plowed through it like an ox, digging where necessary. The bulkhead was completely buried, and he was soon sweaty and hungry from shoveling it out.

Happy, though. Almost buoyant. He barely recognized the feeling. Berron had told him he could have a few days to think over the offer, but when Ti awoke, he knew he would accept it. It scared him, the thought of staying in one place and making a home out of it. Berron would start to know him. He would discover that his blank, beautiful cipher could be moody, insensitive, that when he did speak he often said the wrong thing. At some point he was going to discover that Ti was a wizard, and what then? What was more, if Ti stopped moving, everything that he was and that he'd done might catch up, and he would be forced to know himself again. But, the same things he feared were what made this opportunity tantalizing. He hadn't realized until now how much he missed hearing someone call him by his real name.

When he found the padlock beneath the snow, it was a block of ice. With a quick look around to make sure no one was watching, he took his gloves off, wrapped his fingers around the lock, and quickly thawed it with magic.

The weather had cracked and broken the bulkhead's wooden doors, so the little half-buried compartment of pipes and knobs beyond was full of snow. Ti knelt and used his hands to scoop snow away from the pipes. His fingers hit ice. The whole bottom of the compartment was coated in it. One of the pipes had indeed frozen and burst.

Grimacing, he felt along the painfully cold metal until he found the break. On the backside of the pipe, near the bottom, there was a split. Ice bulged through it, but the pipe was not severely deformed. A plumber could fix it with a coupling, whenever they could get a plumber out here.

Or he could use magic to heat the metal and fuse it back together. It might not be a permanent solution, but it should hold for at least a few more days. No one would ever know.

He wanted that bath.

Ti twisted onto his back in the narrow space. He wrapped his bare fingers around the broken pipe and sent heat into it.

The ice melted under his fingers and dripped cold rivulets down his arms. Ignoring it, he closed his eyes and focused on spreading the heat as far up and down the length of the pipe as he could. He could feel the ice melting and draining—much of it down his arms and into his face.

This was where it got tricky. Gritting his teeth from the exertion and focus the magic required, he took hold of the water within the pipe and held it in place away from where he needed to heat the metal. With his other hand, he called forth a small flame from his palm and directed it against the split in the pipe. If he could get the metal hot enough, he was confident he could coax it to forge itself back together.

The metal around the split began to glow red.

"*Oh!*"

Ti hadn't heard the footsteps approaching in the snow. His heart skipped a beat—the flame went out, and the water gushed free. He jerked upright as cold water sprayed him in the face and squinted into the glare of sunlight.

Berron was looking down at him, his face twisted with horror.

"You're—" he said. "You're a—"

Ti stared at him, speechless, defenseless. He felt his fragile, newborn future wobble on a knife's edge. Slowly, he got to his feet.

Berron stepped back, afraid.

"Berron, wait," Ti said.

The old man darted back through the path Ti had cleared and into the house. Wet and shivering, Ti followed.

Berron stood in the doorway between the kitchen and the hallway, white-faced and clutching the cat to his chest as if to protect it. Ti's bag was at his feet.

"I don't want anything to do with sorcery, lad. I'm a God-fearing man."

"Berron, please," Ti said helplessly. The kitchen was so warm the air burned his lungs. "I won't hurt you. I'm not dangerous."

"I'm sorry," Berron said, his voice tight, "but I think you should go."

"Please," Ti said again. He took a step forward. "I want to stay with you."

Berron lurched back in fright and ended up standing beneath his useless charm. "Ti, please just go—I-I don't want to call the Ordermen."

Ti's temper flared. His real voice hissed out of the dark, ugly place he tried to keep buried. "Go ahead. Call them. Tell them your tavern whore isn't who you thought he was. Do it, you fucking hypocrite."

Berron stared at him. They stood at opposite ends of the kitchen, neither moving. The grandfather clock tick-tocked in the hall.

"Fuck you," Ti said.

With magic, he lifted his bag from Berron's feet and summoned it to him. The old man jumped in fright and twisted his fingers into the Church's hand sign for warding off evil.

It was a slap. It always was. Like he was dirty, inhuman, nothing but vermin to be cast away. He'd been foolish to think he would ever be anything else. Incensed, Ti flung all the cabinets open with magic and smashed every plate and cup and bowl to pieces against the floor. The old man darted into his bedroom with a cry and locked the door.

The kitchen was silent again. The floor was a graveyard of glass and porcelain. Ti took a breath and stamped the anger and hurt down, down. Buried it down deep where the rest of it lived. He summoned Berron's tin of black tea from the counter and the loaf Marius had brought and stowed them in his bag.

Hefting his bag onto his shoulder, he pushed open the door and walked out into the white.

TheraBot

Hannah Frankel

Hannah Frankel lives, works, and writes in Austin, Texas. As a therapist who is also a lifelong lover of science fiction, it was a great pleasure to use this story to explore how her role will change in the society to come. She has been previously published in the Mithila Review.

The Corporate Overlords honored Velma with a bouquet of lilies and a framed certificate for her years of service. That was last month. This month, her supervisor called her into his office and tasked her with programming her replacement.

The day she was given the new assignment, Velma went home and immediately began a period of cramming to rival any from her graduate school era. That next week she remained at home, clicking and reading obsessively about the intersection of clinical psychology and artificial intelligence. On Monday, she sat down ready to answer her own question: What would a good therapist, robot or not, say first?

So on her first day back in the office, she typed into her software, *"Hello [client name], it's very nice to meet you. How are you feeling today?"*

Finally, she exhaled and decided she had earned an ice cream bar, which the Corporate Overlords made freely available in the break room with a spread of other dubious nutritional choices. It was good to be back in the office, if only for the snacks. The project had at least begun.

***

Angie in Customer Support never knew Velma. She would have liked to. She would have been jealous, too. As someone lacking Velma's clout, Angie's own decision to work from home for a week resulted in a pause and, "I'd like you to come in for a one-on-one on Monday."

These meetings cued dread and higher-than-usual anxiety for her. Possibly him too, she reflected, since Brian typically avoided eye contact and mumbled rather than spoke. How Brian had been deemed management material remained a mystery to her.

"Good to see you," she barely made out. "*Hrmpha grmpha grmpha* excellent work you've been doing on the metrics project." Brian always gave compliments before bad news, she had learned.

"However," he continued, "*hrmpha grmpha grrrrmpha* pattern of absenteeism."

"What was that?"

"I said, I'm concerned about your pattern of absenteeism."

"I've been working from home. My back has been flaring up."

"Yes *hrmpha grmpha* work from home policy *hrmpha grmpha*."

Angie had learned that Brian became testy when asked to repeat himself too often, so she only responded, "I understand," although she objectively did not.

"*Hrmpha grmpha* new company wellness policy." He handed her a brochure. "If an employee is deemed to meet criteria of *grrrmpha hrmpha grmpha* require that we provide you a referral to stress management counseling."

She knew she would do it. This job was good enough. Not

lifelong career material, but with her community college diploma Angie wasn't sure what kind of career she was eligible for that she would also want. Angie was not sure of very much, but she was sure that she did not want to be suddenly, unceremoniously unemployed.

"Well, I'll think it over," she said carefully, taking the brochure between thumb and forefinger. "I'm just not sure that I want to talk to some strange person in the company about my private business."

"*Hrmmmmm* not a person, actually."

This did not, in fact, make Angie feel any better.

***

The company's internal research team determined that mental health issues robbed it of over 4,000 person-hours of productivity each year when considering the cumulative effects of increased turnover, leave taken, and diminished output. Growing numbers of employees presented doctors' notes testifying to their depression, anxiety, and the rare bout of psychosis. For years Velma had worked as part of a small department of intra-office mental health "Wellness Consultants," but it was obvious that they were only fighting a rising tide.

Hence, the project that Velma and her colleagues informally dubbed "TheraBot" was hatched. In more formal conversations, the project was known as "JoyCE": the CE stood for Computerized Empathy.

The programmers and user-interface designers assured Velma that she could direct JoyCE to make treatment decisions based on countless variables, woven into complex algorithms. JoyCE could also analyze facial expressions, body posture, vocal pitch and register, and verbal content.

"What about the relationship?" Velma asked, a little desperately, during her initial meeting with the technical team. "Clients need to feel they're being heard and understood, and to register compassion on the face of their treating clinician."

"Oh, yeah." Todd in the rimless glasses nodded with enthusiasm. "That's the easiest part to replicate, actually. Nine out of ten clients couldn't tell the difference with the beta version."

Velma groaned, but she trusted Todd.

The meetings with the technical team she could handle. It was the conjoint management and wellness team meetings that filled her with crazed fantasies of kicking over office furniture and marching out the front door, both middle fingers flying high.

"Do you think you could find a way so that employees won't be required to attend treatment lasting more than six sessions?" piped up one young manager. Probably trying to prove himself, Velma thought. "It's hard on the rest of my team when one of their colleagues has to step away frequently," he continued. "Our numbers are down as a result."

"I can't guarantee anything," said Velma. It had been a long day and her voice was getting shrill. "I can't make JoyCE make people well on any kind of schedule."

"How well does this stuff even work at baseline? What are the outcome statistics with conventional therapy?"

"Depending on the model, most people get significantly better after a few to six months. Better and faster with medication, depending on the diagnosis."

Pause.

"Can we have the robot prescribe medications?"

***

There were no less than three clocks in the small room. Was she being subjected to some kind of reverse Las Vegas-style psychological manipulation? Furthermore, it was hard for Angie to believe the woman in front of her was a robot. She wasn't sleekly beautiful like robot women in movies, but thick-featured with frizzy hair. Looked like she might have a spot of eczema, even.

"Hello, Angie. It's very nice to meet you. How are you feeling today?" the robot asked gently.

"Fine." She was not, in fact, fine. Her back pain really had been flaring up. Ever since her meeting with Brian she had willed herself to trudge into the office anyway, every single morning. She told herself the routine was good for her.

"My name is JoyCE. I've been assigned to work with you."

Pause.

"How are you getting on with work?"

Angie decided to play it straight. "I'm afraid I'll be fired."

"What makes you say that?"

"They told me so."

"What makes you want to continue working here?"

"Because... I have limited options." Angie started to cry,

internally swearing at herself. Crying had not been part of her plan.

"That sounds very hard." JoyCE nodded sympathetically and pushed a box of tissues towards her.

Despite herself, Angie looked forward to her weekly appointments. She was surprised when after six sessions JoyCE thanked Angie for her participation and informed her that they were now at the end of their time together. She would now write her report on whether alternative coping skills had been established, and her recommendation for whether disciplinary or other corrective action should be taken.

"What?" said Angie. "You're going to write a report about me?"

"Yes, it's part of the contract you signed."

"Oh."

Crestfallen and anxious, Angie left that day with a sense of walking to the gallows. Now she was taking her last bus ride home as an employed person. Now she was eating her last plate of microwaveable taquitos as an employed person. She spent a lot of time telling herself it wasn't her fault.

***

Other people seemed to speak their will with an oblivious, strident tone that Velma envied. The young hotshot at the last meeting, for example. He was stupid, true, but she still envied his confidence. In her worst moments, Velma felt like admitting that she had no idea how to make a robot that could help people. She had contributed input towards JoyCE's physical appearance, so she could visualize her now, nodding sympathetically and jotting down notes. But how could she actually help someone navigate crisis?

And yet, she reminded herself of all the days she had recited comforting words by rote. How she had summoned great effort to say the right thing, with a director's eye towards delivery and emphasis. She was an actress for a one-person theater at times. And like an actress, she was a professional who could summon the right procedure regardless of her own internal state.

Apparently, this was the future, and a robot could do her job. The indignity of this realization had worn off. Velma, despite her idealism, was also a pragmatist. However, if she had any say in it, the robot was going to do Velma's job the way Velma wanted her to do it. To get there, though, she would need help.

"Honestly, Todd, I'm worried about this project," she confided after one particularly long meeting. The two of them were alone in the conference room packing up. "There's so much potential to do good, and I get that, but we're marching through a swamp here. The management wants us to scientifically revolutionize mental health treatment, single-handedly. And I'm not sure I think that's responsible, or kind, when a lot of people's jobs are on the line."

Todd twisted his lips and nodded. "I have reservations about their priorities. You know that."

"Exactly," she said emphatically. "This isn't about long-term individual wellness, this is about patching in a modicum of support which, if unsuccessful, conveniently leaves an HR paper trail."

She explained her preferred personal treatment approach, and how she thought this could best be translated to JoyCE.

"It could get us both fired," he grinned. "If we weren't both about to retire. I might even be able to make it look like a glitch or a mistake. It won't last forever, but it will take them a few years to figure it out if we're lucky."

Velma grinned back. "The world is an imperfect place. But a few years is a lot of people's jobs. Especially if they're only coming for 6 sessions at a time."

***

Angie left Brian's office dumbstruck, still clutching the report that elucidated her motivation, skills mastery, and--wonder of wonders--"positive attitude." She requested JoyCE's soonest opening for an emergency session on the online portal. By the time she crossed the office threshold, she decided that a "no bullshit" approach was again best.

"Why did you write this?"

"It was my assessment. I believe you'll make good use of it."

"I can't believe you would do this for me. Thank you so, so much." Angie was breathless and, once again, tearing up.

"You're welcome. But really, you deserve it. I'm only doing my job."

Near the end of their allotted time, JoyCE sighed and looked pointedly at the clock. "One last thing we need to touch on." She pushed a business card across the table. "Here's a referral for a career counselor. Please, Angie, don't put this one off."

Angie had the good sense to finish out her time at the company without asking too many questions. But if she had been able to read the report that came out some time later, the one that killed the JoyCE project, she would have discovered that she was in fact the beneficiary of a great, merciful mistake. At least, that was one version.

As was written up in that report, JoyCE rarely recommended termination, seeming instead to perpetually lean towards "another chance" in all but the most egregious cases. What the report did not say outright was that JoyCE had been running buried programs calculating the outcome of management decisions, and only recommended termination in cases where the decision was a foregone one. She could determine this from the rate of absenteeism, deplorable productivity or quality metrics, and textual analysis of manager e-mail communication regarding the employee.

***

Our real heroine, like most, reaped only quiet rewards. Yet Velma was satisfied nonetheless. The JoyCE project had recently launched and was deemed a modest success. Her retirement party served cake and veggie platters, accompanied by short formulaic speeches and earnest gratitude expressed in smaller circles.

"It's time to go," she said simply when asked about the possibility of ongoing contract work. "Besides, I have a lot of faith in the JoyCE project. In the past, I worried about how much compassion a robot could offer, but she and I both have surprised ourselves." People say a lot of nice things they don't necessarily mean at retirement parties, but Velma absolutely meant this.

The Truth as Written
J.S. Rogers

J.S. has been writing since she could get her hands on a pencil and paper. These days, she writes as a freelancer for her day job and pens fiction by night. Her fiction has appeared in print and around the web.

Everyone in Mountain View knew that Miss Minuet's store was the most interesting thing in town. Minuet claimed she sold magical goods and services from her little store-front right off of main street, and maybe she did. Certainly strange people often stopped in Mountain View just to visit her, usually leaving with some little package wrapped in plain brown paper.

The locals usually left her alone. Miss Minuet tended to charge high prices for items that couldn't possibly do the things she said they could do. The Saturday morning that Claire pushed through the front door, listening to the bell chime overhead and holding onto Maggie's hand, she wasn't planning to buy anything.

Her parents were busy, again, leaving her with the weekend free to do what she wanted. What she wanted mostly to do was add something from Miss Minuet's store to her collection. Over the last year or so, she'd managed to take something from every other store in Mountain View without getting caught. The only business left was Miss Minuet's Magical Goods and More.

Maggie usually accompanied her on these outings. Maggie's big, wide eyes and easy smile did a great job of distracting clerks and store owners, while Claire went about her business. Maggie had protested, at first, but she'd fully embraced the entire challenge after the previous year. Claire knew Maggie was using it as a distraction after her father's death. She didn't particularly mind.

Maggie gave her hand a last squeeze, moving over to the counter, where Miss Minuet was watching them both with a scowl. Miss Minuet didn't have many wrinkles, but the ones she had were deep and set into place. Her hair was steel grey and always pulled back harshly. Her voice suggested that she only drank whiskey and spent a fair amount of time eating cigars. She acknowledged Maggie's greeting with a little grunt.

Claire left them to it, slipping down a tightly packed aisle. There were boxes and jars, many of them labeled in languages Claire couldn't read. Pleasant smells wafted from some of them. Others stank terribly. They were all too big for her purposes.

She began to despair of finding anything that would work as she moved through the store, until she exited an aisle and found a display case left open. There was a cardboard box beside it, full of packing material. An invoice lay to one side. Claire lifted it up, snorting a little at the order for one pen, magical. A note on the invoice promised that the pen would write only the truth.

Claire wasn't sure what use a pen that would only write the truth would be, but the writing instrument was right there, on a little stand in the case. It would easily fit in her pocket. She could probably hide it in her hand, if necessary.

She smiled, lifted it, stuffed it in her pocket, and turned on her heel.

"You about done?" she asked Maggie, as she reached the front door.

Maggie said, "In just a minute, you run on ahead." It was their normal code. They'd found the process worked best if Maggie stayed behind a few minutes to throw off suspicion. Claire turned towards home, only a few streets away, to wait for Maggie and get a better look at her new trophy.

***

So, Claire ended up with a pen that could, supposedly, only write the truth. She took it out of her pocket back in her bedroom, turning it over and over. It was heavy and made of some kind of metal, cool against her fingers when she gripped it. She couldn't see a seam on it; she wasn't sure how they'd gotten the ink in, but it wrote when she scribbled on a piece of paper.

She shrugged, looking at the ink, and wrote: *My name is Claire.*

The words were true and the pen seemed to have no trouble displaying them. It didn't magically improve her handwriting, that was for sure. She tapped the paper a few times, leaving behind little smears of ink, and wrote, to test it: *My eyes are blue.*

Claire's eyes were a brown so dark they looked almost black in all but the brightest lighting. Nevertheless, the pen dutifully wrote out the words. She sighed. She hadn't really believed that a pen could tell what was true and what wasn't, so she wasn't disappointed as she scrawled out a number of other lies, before crumpling up the paper, and throwing it away.

At least she hadn't wasted any money on the pen.

She was preparing to drop it in a drawer when Maggie tapped on her window, her cheeks red and a smile on her face. Claire opened the window and Maggie climbed through, rolled across the bed, and landed on her feet, long practiced in this method of ingress. "I can't believe you took it," Maggie said, laughing. "I was sure she was going to see you!"

"She might as well have," Claire said, rolling her eyes. "It doesn't work, anyway. It was supposed to only write the truth, but it doesn't."

"Are you sure?" Maggie said, some of the giddy joy leaving her expression. "Maybe you're doing it wrong."

"I'm sure." Claire waved the pen around and pulled one of the crumpled papers from the trash. She flattened it across her desk and said, "Look." She wrote, a quick, inelegant scrawl: *Maggie isn't here.* "See?"

She looked up, gesturing with the paper and found her room empty. There'd been no sound of the door opening. The window was down. But Maggie wasn't there anymore. Something cold ran down the back of Claire's neck. She stood up, turning in a fast circle, as though maybe Maggie was just lurking behind her shoulder.

"Maggie?" She ducked down, looking under the bed, though that space was just as full of junk as it had been last night. "Maggie, this isn't funny." She pulled open the closet, then the door to her bedroom, looking out into the hall.

Everything was quiet. She still held the pen, gripped tight in her hand. She stared down at the words and, in a sudden panic, crossed them out.

She looked around; still no sign of Maggie. "I'm serious, you're scaring me," she said, to an empty room and terrible silence. She shuddered and wrote: *Maggie is here.*

And suddenly, Maggie was there, collapsing down onto the floor, her arms and legs shaking, her eyes rolled back in her head. Claire screamed, not intending to, backing up, and knocking her desk chair over. Maggie jerked across the carpet, her lips gone blue, something dark and wet running out of her nose. She was making a terrible, low, groaning sound.

Claire fell to her knees and scrambled towards Maggie, trying to remember what you did when someone had a seizure. Were you supposed to hold them still, put something in their mouth so they couldn't bite off their tongue? Roll them onto their right side? She couldn't remember, even as she grabbed Maggie's shoulders.

Maggie felt cold as ice, even through her clothes. She was shaking her head, violently, back and forth. She thrashed her arms out, catching the side of Claire's head, knocking her back. Claire scrambled away, pushing with her heels, grabbing for the paper on the desk and scrawling: *Maggie is okay.*

Maggie went still, all at once. She flopped down, onto her back, staring up at the ceiling, her breath wheezing in her throat. "Hey," Claire said, quietly. Her heart wouldn't slow down. Maggie didn't say anything. Claire edged closer and leaned over her. "Hey, are you—"

And that was when Maggie started screaming, like she was dying, being murdered right there on Claire's floor. She thrashed, bringing her arms up and clawing at her face, no, her eyes. Claire reeled back once more, horror making it difficult to think before she reached for the wall, a clean area of paint, and wrote, in a hurried rush, desperate to do anything to stop the screaming: *Maggie is the way she was before she climbed through the window.*

Maggie wasn't on the floor anymore. Claire watched her just blink away, disappearing. She left behind smears of red blood across the carpet. As Claire stared at it, there was a knock on her window. She turned, slowly, and stared at Maggie's smiling face, her cheeks reddened from excitement, as the bottom fell out of Claire's stomach.

***

"It works," Claire said, her voice flat and coming from far away, as Maggie tumbled into her room again.

"What works?" Maggie asked, brushing herself off and looking around the room. "Why were you writing on the wall?"

"This pen. It said it wrote only true things." Claire waved it through the air. "But it doesn't only write things that are true. It writes anything, but if the thing isn't true, it *makes* it true."

"That doesn't make any sense," Maggie said, and Claire laughed, flat. The sound drew a concerned look from Maggie, who added, "Why don't you tell me what's going on?" So, Claire did, turning the pen over and over in her fingers as she tried to explain and, at the end, Maggie said, "Alright, ha ha, you really had me going there."

Claire curled her shoulders over and wrote, on her hand: *Maggie believes me.*

"Oh, man," Maggie said, shifting around on the bed, "you're really serious, aren't you? Well, what are we going to do?" She looked so earnest. So concerned. Claire had made her that way, changed her inside with just a few letters.

Bile burned up the back of Claire's throat, bitter and terrible. "I don't know. I—I think I changed some things, already." She'd written a bunch of lies, to test the pen. She swore, grabbing at the trash-can and pulling it over, grabbing the crumpled papers, flattening them hurriedly across the table.

Her eyes were probably blue now, she realized. And she was a straight-A student, perhaps. And she'd been accepted into her college of choice with a full scholarship. These were all lies she could fix, she thought. Maybe she didn't even need to fix all of them. Who cared how she got into college, really?

She noticed Maggie drifting closer out of the corner of her eye and looked up in time to watch Maggie lift the pen, turn it over, and then grab for a paper. "What are you doing?" Claire demanded, grabbing for the pen. "It's not safe, you can't—"

My father is alive, Maggie had written in her smooth, flowing cursive. She looked around Claire's bedroom, expectantly. Claire gripped her wrist, squeezing tight. "You can't use it. Weren't you listening to me? It isn't safe. It does things you don't expect."

Maggie gave her a strange, dreamy look. Her eyes weren't focusing, really. She said, "Just because you wrote stupid things doesn't mean there's something wrong with the pen. We just have to think before we use it."

"I am thinking!" Claire tried to pry the pen from Maggie's hand, but Maggie hit her, then, across the face, and she reeled backwards, holding her nose. Her eyes watered from the sudden pain. She tasted something sharp and salty in the back of her throat. She blinked her eyes clear in time to watch Maggie write something else on the paper. "What are you doing? Stop!"

Claire would have yelled more, but there was a sudden, terrible smell in the room, and a creaking groan. The hair on her arms rose. She turned her head, her hands still up by her face, and screamed. There was a dead man, in her room. Or, technically, maybe he was alive. He was rotting, though. Pieces of him were missing. He smelled of formaldehyde and decay. She recognized him as Maggie's father, dead and buried for months now.

He clawed clumsily at his jaw. Didn't they wire your jaw together, after you died, to make sure that you looked nice in the coffin? He groaned in his chest, taking a shuffling step towards them, and Claire jerked back, running into the wall, trying to propel herself up with no success. She looked around; he was between her and the door. He even blocked the window.

Maggie was staring at him, her face bone-white and her eyes wide, her mouth moving soundlessly. She still held the pen in one hand. Claire lunged for it, shoving her onto the bed, pinning her arm to the mattress and yanking the pen from her grip with no gentleness. *Mr. Hawthorne is dead again,* she wrote, and, when she heard a dull thud on her floor, she continued, *dead and back in his grave just like he was like this never happened.*

For a moment she couldn't bring herself to look around, convinced that there would still be a body in the middle of her floor. But it had gone, leaving another terrible stain behind on her carpet. She still held Maggie down, but there was no more fight left in her. Maggie just lay there, curled onto her side, weeping.

"I'm sorry," Claire said. Her nose felt stuffy. She still tasted blood in her mouth. "I'm—"

Maggie only cried harder, kicking out at Claire, until Claire had no choice but to retreat, scrambling off of the bed. Maggie curled herself into a ball, wrapping her arms up around her head, while Claire thought of the other things she'd written, about her brother never being able to talk to her again, about her ex dying in a fire, and all of it was horrible.

She stared at the pen. The ink was staining her fingers. She'd written so many things into being. She doubted any of them had caused anything but pain. But there had to be some kind of way to put things to rights.

She knew she needed to think about it, to make sure that she didn't make another mistake, but she couldn't bear to delay. Everything that she had done needed to be undone. She had to fix it, fix all of it, make sure that Maggie never ended up curled up on her blankets, crying like she was dying or like she'd rather be dead.

She looked down at her bare forearm and wrote, the ink flowing smoothly across her skin: *I got caught trying to take the pen from Minuet's Magical Goods and More.*

***

Claire reached out for the pen, confident that Maggie had effectively engaged Miss Minuet in a conversation about nothing. It was Maggie's greatest gift. She'd tuck the little thing into her pocket, head home, and they could laugh over the ridiculousness of a magical pen together. She'd almost grabbed it when someone cleared their throat directly behind her.

She turned slowly in place, plastering a smile on her face as she looked over at Miss Minuet, who frowned up at her with one eyebrow arched severely. "And what do you think you've been doing, missy?" Minuet asked, her voice that rough, whiskey-and-tobacco rasp.

"Nothing," Claire said, holding onto her bright smile. "Just looking around. You've got some crazy stuff in here."

"I do," Miss Minuet said, "but it's all for paying customers only, so why don't you two girls run along now? I'm sure you've got better things to do than mock an old woman."

"Oh, we would never," Claire said, but she relented, heading towards the door. She had no idea how the old woman had seen her, but she knew when she was busted. She gave Maggie a sour look as she headed towards the door, and Maggie shrugged back at her, apologetic. They slipped through the door, the day stretching before them.

As they left, the little bell jingling, she thought she heard Miss Minuet saying, "Now, what have you been up to? Misbehaving, I see." She made a tsking sound as the door shut.

"Crazy old bat," Maggie said, hooking her arm through Claire's. "But, still, there's some weird stuff in there, Claire. I'm kind of glad you didn't take anything. Let's just head over to the park. Get an ice cream."

Claire rolled her eyes, but good-naturedly. She hadn't even realized that the hair was standing up on the back of her neck until they stepped out of the store and her heart-rate started to slow. She turned them towards the park, swallowing to get rid of a weird, coppery taste in her mouth, and the afternoon reached out to enfold them.

THANK YOU TO OUR SUPPORTERS

Many thanks to our patrons and supporters, especially:

Anna O'Brien • Cathrin Hagey • Kathryn Parsons
Natalie Weizenbaum • Johanna Levene

Matthew Bennardo • Aidan Long • Anna Evans
Bonnie Warford • carol shoemake
D.M. Domosea • Erik DeBill • Felicia OSullivan
J'nae Spano • Katie Conrad • Kennon Hulett
Martin Cohen • Mollie Morgeson • Salomao Becker
Tory Hoke • Steven • Frederick Stark

Ally Shaw • BethOfAus • Brit Hvide • Carly Racklin
Charlotte Nash-Stewart • Dirck de Lint • Emily Anderson
GriffinFire • J. Askew • Jen G • Jocelyn Actual
Karen Anderson • Kayla • Kristina Saccone • Leslie Anderson
Liz Warner • Maria Haskins • Rochelle B • Sian Jones
Suzanne Thackston • Wanda • willowcabins

Want to see your name here? Become a patron!
patreon.com/lunastation

ⓟ patreon

About the Cover Artist

Eleonor is a Portuguese Illustrator and Character Concept Artist.

She is interested in characters most of all, and good stories within rich worlds with extensive lore filled with mystery. In her work, she loves to play with iconography, fashion, textures and composition, to create poignant and visually appealing images full of symbolism.

Her playgrounds of choice are Sci-fi and Fantasy, and the places where both meet.

She has painted illustrations and characters for a number of tabletop role-playing games, as well as book covers, and would like to one day add costume design for films and concept art for video-games to that list.

Guillermo del Toro shared her fanart of The Shape of Water on Twitter, and might have changed the canon of the movie to accommodate it. Possibly. Maybe. Or at least he thought about it.

She's based near Lisbon, Portugal.

You can find more of her work at:

https://eleonorpiteira.carbonmade.com

NOW AVAILABLE!

THE BEST OF
LUNA STATION QUARTERLY
THE FIRST FIVE YEARS

Featuring fifty stories by emerging women writers, with cover art by Hugo award-winner Julie Dillon

Luna Station Press is proud to celebrate the fifth anniversary of our flagship Quarterly with this special anthology.

The writers gathered in these pages, from every corner of the globe, are explorers of wonder, magic, and places beyond the stars. They are also explorers of what makes us human, in heart, mind, and spirit.

Come explore the best we have to offer, as we look back fondly on the last five year and look ahead at what's to come.

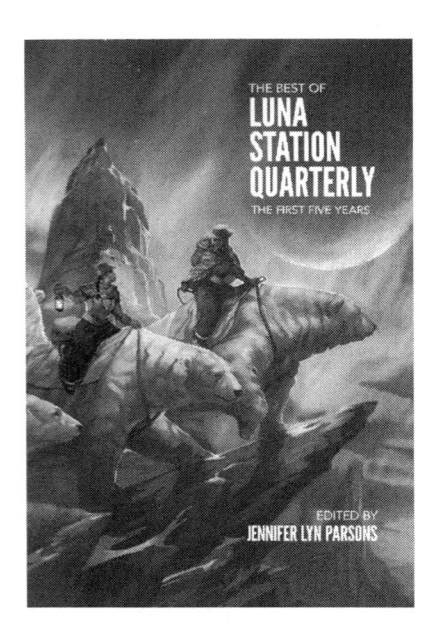

LUNA STATION PRESS

Printed in Poland
by Amazon Fulfillment
Poland Sp. z o.o., Wrocław